Home to Brushy Creek

Home to Brushy Creek

The War Was Over But Ward Still Had Some Battles to Fight

Howard R. Bratton

iUniversity Press
San Jose New York Lincoln Shanghai

Home to Brushy Creek
The War Was Over But Ward Still Had Some Battles to Fight

iUniversity Press
an imprint of iUniverse.com, Inc.

For information address:
iUniverse.com, Inc.
5220 S 16th, Ste. 200
Lincoln, NE 68512
www.iuniverse.com

It's all fiction.

ISBN: 0-595-15153-1

Printed in the United States of America

Acknowledgements

Thanks to my dear wife for her help and patience which went way beyond her marriage vows. I also want to thank my son, Keith, for his help in getting the manuscript submitted.

Chapter 1

Glad to see another ex-soldier in Union blue, Ward ambled over to the table where the young veteran was sitting all by himself, and said, "Mind if I join you?"

The ex-trooper took another swig from his glass then nodded toward a chair. Ward pulled it out, set his glass on the table and introduced himself.

"My name is Garrison…Ward Garrison."

It was while he was seating himself that he noticed the crutch on the floor beside the young veteran's chair.

The raw-boned young trooper stuck his hand out, and said, "I'm Bill Sessions. Are you kin to the Garrison clan here in Marlin? I don't remember seein' you around."

"Yeah, I'm one of them," Ward smiled, "but my dad and mom left Marlin for Texas back in '41. I was born there and grew up there. I just stopped by on my way home for a visit…you live around here?"

"Yeah, born and raised here…never been anywhere before they put me in the Army."

"I see you had a bit of bad luck," Ward sympathized.

"Yeah, lost it at Shiloh fightin' in another feller's place."

"You mean some feller who hired you to go in his place?"

"That's right…want me to tell you who it was?"

"I hope it wasn't a Garrison…"

"It sure was…Evan Garrison, Jr." Bill let him have it straight out.

"I'm sorry to hear that," Ward said, feeling a little let down. "I know it won't change things, but you are lookin' at a Garrison that fought through four years of th' bloody hell, and I'm as proud of having done my part as I am put out at any Garrison for not doing his."

"OK," Bill said, "I'm sorry I dropped it on you like that.…But while we are on the subject, you might as well know that he was not the only Marlin Garrison who hired himself a substitute. In fact, every one of them of fightin' age hired a man to go in his place."

"Well, Bill," Ward replied, hoping to put an end to any further discussion of the Garrison family's lack of patriotism, "I've told you how I feel about it.…Even though it was legal and nobody was forced to be a substitute, it was a shameful thing to do. I hope every man who did it can live it down, especially the Garrisons."

"You say nobody was forced?" Bill's face got red and his voice started rising, "let me tell you, when your ol' daddy and two uncles with big families to raise, will be fired if you won't let yourself be hired, that comes mighty close t' bein' forced!"

"You mean Evan just stood by and let his daddy do that?" Ward couldn't believe it. If the ex-soldier was telling the truth, there had to be a good reason…

"You bet he did," Bill promptly assured him. "Oh, his pa gave me an extra hundred to salve his conscience, but it was still th' next thing to bein' forced."

"Yeah, I guess it was," Ward admitted. He then went on to ask, "Has he or Evan offered anything extra for your…ah, loss?"

"Offer me something extra! Ha!" Bill scoffed, "they want even hire me back to work for them! They say a one-legged man can't get around well enough to do the kind of work they want done."

"Bill," Ward said, "I wish I could help you, but since I have not yet met any of my Marlin kin folks, I can't make any promises. But if I get a chance, I'll see what I can do…"

"Ah, don't worry about it," Bill said, "even if you wasn't wearin' Yankee blue I doubt if you could do me any good. Don't be too surprised if you're not welcomed with open arms. Some folks around here believe—without sayin' much, of course— that the Garrisons liked Confederate gray much more than they did Yankee blue."

Ward was taken aback. But he didn't respond in any hostile way to the veteran's defamatory words. He'd been taking some big swigs from his glass and it could be the whiskey talking.

Instead of taking offense, he tried to leave him with a better outlook on things by saying, "Bill, I'm sorry you had such bad luck. But don't give up. I know a couple of old cowhands down in Texas who are still doin' a full day's work with just one leg…somebody will hire you."

"Well, I don't know," Bill started feeling sorry for himself, "while I'm off doin' someone else's fightin', my girl marries one of my cousins and they run off to Canada so he won't have to join up.…And now, besides not bein' able to find work, I can't even find a girl who'll take up with a one-legged man. Hell! Even th' whores in th' whorehouse want t' charge me double!"

Chapter 2

Just as thousands of other war-weary soldiers had done, Ward mustered himself out of the army the next day after the long, bloody struggle had finally ended. From Richmond he had hoboed his way to Springfield in central Illinois, but from there to Marlin in the southern part of the state, he had been a paying passenger on a stagecoach.

He had arrived in Marlin about noon…which was nearly two weeks after he had ridden his old cavalry charger through Richmond on his way to the railhead north of that subdued but once proud city. He had written his grandmother five weeks earlier that he was planning to stop by to see her when the long drawn out struggle was finally over.

He had put another letter in the mail the day before he left telling her that he was on his way. But with all of the uncertainties of travel he, of course, could not tell her exactly when he would be arriving. So when the stagecoach arrived in Marlin he was not surprised when no one was waiting to greet him. But it was just as well because he needed some time to "rinse the road dust out of his throat" and make himself more presentable.

That was how he came to be in the barroom seated at a table with the bitter young veteran who was feeling sorry for himself. Bill was still muttering something about the Garrisons not doing him right, when Ward wished him better days and got up to leave. He had paid both of their tabs at the bar, and had then gone out to find a barbershop.

He'd found one just down the street where he'd bought himself a dollar's worth of almost forgotten "civilian amenities". And while he was getting a hot-lather shave, a haircut and a hot bath, his other uniform was being brushed, spot-cleaned and pressed.

As he was getting dressed in the back room he wondered if he should pin his captain's bars back on....He knew he had damn well earned them and he was proud of them. But he was sure some folks, even relatives, might find it hard to believe that he'd been made a captain when he was only twenty-two.

It occurred to him that he might be looked on as more of a stranger than a family member by the relatives he had never seen. As a matter of fact, he remembered very few letters his daddy had received from the family he had left behind. —None at all during the past several years except the one that told of his father's death some six years back.

He finally decided to leave the bars off. After all—in spite of what his drinking companion had said about Garrison men hiring substitutes— some of his uncles or cousins might have served without making it to officer rank. In which case he didn't want them to think he was showing off. Rather than presume that he'd be immediately accepted as one of the family, it might be better if he, at first anyway, behaved more like a guest.

As he was slipping into his jacket he noticed that he felt no real pain in the shoulder that had caught some Reb's miniball just four days before the shooting had stopped. He windmilled his arm a couple of times and felt no pain he couldn't stand without flinching. He didn't want to be seen favoring an arm as if he was looking for pity.

He wrapped his gun belt around his old horse pistol and stowed it in his duffel bag. The old cap-and-ball muzzle-loader had served him well. But he hoped he would never have to use it again...but of course he was still a long way from home and the peace and quiet of good old Brushy Creek.

He tipped the shine boy, put his hat on and glanced at himself in the mirror. After having worn a beard for a year, he was a little startled by the fresh trimmed, clean shaved bucko that was looking back at him. But he was pleased by his overall appearance: Tall, fully matured, wide shoulders, slim waist, blue eyes, brick-red hair, square jaw…

He was not out to make a handsome-soldier impression on anybody, but looking one's best shouldn't be held against a young man who was aiming to carve out an empire in Texas, and start mixing and mingling with some of the state's most important people.

With his duffel bag slung from his shoulder, he strolled down to the first cross street, turned the corner and spotted the big sign that he had glimpsed from the stagecoach an hour or so before. The big sign proudly identified the three-story building that took up most of the block as being: THE GARRISON MERCANTILE BUILDING.

He had seen a number of flags around town flying at half-mast in remembrance of President Lincoln who had been killed by a crazy, hate-filled actor. But there were no Stars and Stripes flying on the top of the big Garrison building. He shrugged his shoulders and assumed that somebody had just forgot to run it up.

The big brass door yielded to a surprisingly easy push, and he stepped inside the biggest place of business he'd ever seen in his life: Neatly arranged displays of merchandise from wall-to wall and floor to ceiling everywhere he looked. All of that plus, as a sign pointed out, FURNITURE and HOUSEWARES on the second floor.

An old clerk with stooped shoulders, watery eyes and a carnation in his lapel met him just inside the door.

"I'm looking for one of the Mr. Garrisons," Ward told the old hireling.

"Right this way, Sir," he respectfully replied. The courteous old clerk was respectful in a way that no doubt pleased a lot customers and kept them coming back.

The mannerly old gentleman led him up two flights of stairs, down a long carpeted hallway and stopped at a highly polished oaken door that had the name EVAN GARRISON, JR. lettered upon it in big gold letters. He stepped up to it, squared up his shoulders and tapped lightly—exactly twice.

"Enter," a man's voice seemed to command more than invite.

The old clerk opened the door, and with almost formal decorum announced: "A gentleman to see you, Sir."

"Yes?" Evan, Jr. inquired with a brief glance as the door closed behind the old menial.

"I'm Ward Garrison," Ward introduced himself with a big Texas smile, "and we must be cousins," he went on as he stepped forward and offered his hand for a friendly shake.

"Well, I guess we could be," Evan, Jr. responded with a lack of interest that was close to being downright discourteous, "if you are the son of John Garrison who lives in Texas…I know all of my other cousins."

With just enough civility to barely hide his ill grace, Evan finally got to his feet, leaned across his big symbol of power and status and offered his pudgy hand for an indifferent handshake.

Ward couldn't resist making the pompous bastard pay for his ill manners. He crushed his dough-soft hand in a Texas handshake that left his haughty cousin's fingers stinging as if he had just jerked them out of a beehive.

"Well," Ward said when he finally let go of his toplofty cousin's pudgy hand, "I was just passin' through and thought I'd drop by for a visit. How's our grandmother?…I would especially like to visit with her."

"She's just fine," Evan's mumbled reply was almost a moan.

Ward smiled as he watched his uppity cousin rub his fingers against the seat of his pants.

Evan finally reseated himself and went on to say, "If you want to go out to the house to visit with her, Bailey, the old clerk you just saw, will give you directions."

And with those words Ward's bumptious young cousin-executive reached for some papers and started shuffling them around. He pursed his lips and wrinkled his brow as he "studied" first one then another as if the future of Garrison Enterprises was hanging in the balance, waiting for another one of his brilliant, company-saving decisions.

After four years in the army Ward knew when he was being dismissed. He stopped just short of clicking his heels and snapping off a sarcastic salute. Instead, he maintained his civility, and said, "I'll be seein' you…"

After quietly closing the door behind him, he went back down the stairs to find the old clerk. He was sure he'd be getting a much warmer welcome from his grandmother…

*   *   *

At the end of a dusty, mile-long hike on a road that was plainly marked as being strictly private, he was surprised to find himself standing in front of a very pretentious, plantation style house. It reminded him of some he'd seen in a once posh district of Richmond. But there was no paint peeling from the gleaming white front of this one, and there was no dead limb propping up a rose trellis in the formal garden so beautifully situated in a far corner of the spacious lawn.

He wondered if he could have misunderstood the old clerk's directions? But no, the artfully lettered sign he'd seen hanging from the arm of the little black jockey, had plainly stated that this was GARRISON MANOR.

A broad, redbrick walk led from the roadside up to a grand veranda that was elegantly laid with big red tiles that matched the bricks in the walk. Five tall columns that rose from the veranda to support a full-width second-floor balcony accented the front of the grand abode.

Six hesitant steps took him across the veranda's polished red tiles to the big front door. He lifted the big brass knocker and let it fall. He immediately realized that he had lifted it way too high, and had made an unseemly racket. To show that he knew better, he lifted it again and tapped lightly.

After nearly a minute he was about to tap again, but the massive door was swung back and he found himself facing a middle-aged black man in full butler's garb…long, swallow-tailed black coat, gray pants, white gloves, the whole "nine yards".

"Yes, Suh. What can I do for you?" the spruced up manservant inquired in a quite formal manner.

"I'm Ward Garrison," Ward informed him, "I've come to see Mrs. Garrison."

"Yes, Suh," the butler said, as he took Ward's hat and stepped back to let him enter, "wait right here and I'll go tell her."

The stiff-backed butler disappeared at the end of a long hallway, leaving Ward to gape in wide-eyed wonder at all the finery he'd stepped into. There was a thirty-foot Persian rug on the floor, a marble mantel that must have been made in Italy. . . fine chairs and two couches all upholstered in silk, and side tables all topped with marble. And to set it all off, rising before him was the biggest, grandest staircase he'd ever laid eyes on. Neither of his parents had ever even hinted that the Marlin Garrisons had lived in such fine style.

He hadn't expected anyone to appear on the elegant staircase or anywhere else so soon. There had to be one of those speaking tubes somewhere in the back of the house, because all of a sudden a youngish woman in a black silk dress was standing at the head of the elegantly curving stairway. He saw at once that she was at least twenty years too young to be his grandmother.

He smiled, and said, "I'm Ward Garrison, John Garrison's son. I'm here to visit my grandmother…you must be one of my aunts."

The woman looked him up and down with a cool smile, and without coming on down the stairs, she said, "John never told you, did he?…I'm your step-grandmother. Your grandmother died two months before John married Laura and the two of them left for Texas."

Ward was naturally at a loss for words, but he finally stammered, "W…well, no, he didn't. I…I'm sorry to come bargin' in here like this."

"That's all right…from your letter, I guessed you didn't know. My name is Emily." All of her words were spoken with little warmth and conveyed no real sign of welcome.

"I'm glad to get to know you," Ward said, "I wonder if you could tell me how I might find one or two of my uncles?"

While continuing to stand at the head of the grand staircase, Emily pondered his request for a moment, and then said, "Yes, but I think I have a better idea—one that will save you some time and a lot of running around. I'll invite everybody over this evening for dinner—there is still plenty of time—and you can visit with them here."

"That's mighty kind of you, Ma'am," Ward accepted her offer, "I'm obliged to you.…Meanwhile I'll get a room at the hotel and do some restin' up."

Emily nodded, and said, "I'll ask everybody to be here at seven.…Johnson," she called out, "have Ike bring a buggy around and take Mr. Garrison to the hotel."

"Yassum," the butler answered from somewhere in the back of the "Garrison Manor".

"Thank you again, Ma'am," Ward said, "I'll be looking forward to seein' everybody."

His step-grandmother nodded from the head of the stairs, and Ward knew that he was again being dismissed by a Marlin Garrison.

*   *   *

"Ike," Ward asked the old hostler as the high-stepping bay drew the buggy along at a right pert clip, "how long have you been with Miss Emily?"

"Oh, Suh," he replied, "I guess it's nigh on to twenty-five years now."

"You escaped out of slavery and came north?"

"Oh, no, Suh. Miz Emily, she brung me up from Erin, Tennessee soon afta she married Mistuh Garrison."

Ward wondered if Emily had told Ike that he was no longer a slave. Surely the old slave had heard…there was probably some wage agreement now. He didn't ask…he was willing to give "Miz" Emily the benefit of the doubt.

*   *   *

He took the key from the desk clerk, and went up to his room to sprawl out on the bed. He needed to do some thinking…

Why had his daddy not told him about his grandmother? Why had his cousin, Evan Jr., been so unfriendly? For that matter, why had his step-grandmother been so cool?

Had the grand, plantation-style house been Emily's idea, or his grandfather Andy's? It was too new to be the original Garrison house. And why was there no black bow on Emily's front door when every other house he had seen was displaying one in sad remembrance of a great president?

It had been a long day. He was too weary to try to figure it all out. Maybe he'd get some answers to his questions at the big evening get- together.

Chapter 3

Not wanting to wear more blisters on his feet, Ward rented a big bay at the livery stable for an easy canter out to the big evening get-together.

He tethered the big gelding to the hitching rack out by the carriage shed, crossed the wide lawn on the neatly edged pathway, stepped up on the grand veranda and walked on over to the big door with its brass knocker. This time he was careful not to let the heavy knocker drop so "indecorously".

Johnson, the duded-up butler, let him in and closed the big door behind him. He then led him through a side door into a dining room that could accommodate a two-fiddle, Saturday night barn dance with room to spare. As the butler retreated with a slight bow, the frontier boy from Texas was left facing at least two dozen Garrisons seated around a long, elegantly-set dining table that was dazzling to behold…

Candles flickering in silver candle holders…fresh, neatly arranged flowers in cut-glass vases…long stem wineglasses glistening in the light from the flickering candles…linen napkins big as saddle blankets, and an array of fancy silverware like some he'd once seen in a pawn shop. Everything that could sparkle was sparkling under a huge crystal chandelier with at least one hundred candles arranged in a big pyramid upon it. It must've taken Johnson an hour to light them all up.

If his step-grandmother had purposely set out to do it, she could not have done a better job of intimidating him…he had gone into battles feeling a lot less nervous. With everybody's gaze fixed upon him, he felt more like he'd been called in to face a court martial than to have a get-acquainted dinner with kinfolk.

He spotted Miss Emily at the far end of the table all decked out in another elegant black dress. Her dark hair had been perfectly coifed, and her still-young face had been made up to enhance her naturally attractive features. He lifted his hand and started to say, "Hi", but she spoke first.

"Good evening," she nodded coolly and immediately started her introductions. "Ward," she said, "that is Glen Garrison, the youngest of your uncles, seated there by you at the end of the table."

When his Uncle Glen quickly accepted Ward's hand in kinship, Emily said, "Let's leave off the handshakes for now, and let me just tell him everybody's name." Which she went on to do, stating each person's relationship…whether blood-kin, an in-law, an invited friend, or fiancée.

Finally, when he had exchanged nods with the last one, she curtly advised, "The chair there to Glen's left is for you."

As he was seating himself he took another quick look at Maggie Carson, the girl who'd been introduced as Evan, Jr's fiancée.

He was surprised when he saw that she was boldly gazing at him. He looked away but in the brief moment his eyes were on her he saw that her eyes were as green as Texas clover in springtime, and her hair—as black as a raven's wing—was hanging to her shoulders in unruly waves.

He didn't think she could be judged as being downright beautiful, but there was an allure about her that would immediately attract the attention of any "drawing room Casanova". He couldn't see enough of her body to form any fair judgement there, but there was no hint of a double chin and her hands were trim and nicely shaped.

She had been the only person at the table besides his Uncle Glen who had smiled with any warmth when they were introduced. But with her being Evan, Jr's fiancée he immediately curbed any thought of getting to know her in a romantic way.

Someone at Emily's end of the table gave thanks for the "bountiful meal", and three black maids began serving.

While the maids were serving the soup, his Uncle Glen looked at him, and said, "None of us Marlin Garrisons could be spared to do any fighting....But we did our part here at home running businesses that supported the war effort...making leather for boots, saddles and harnesses; growing wheat, milling flour; providing horses, mules, and beef cattle...

"We provided the army with more than five thousand horses and pack mules...bought most of them in Missouri and Kentucky, fattened them up a bit, and resold them to the army at a fair profit. You may have ridden one of the horses."

Ward couldn't resist saying, with a grim smile, "I may have ridden four of them since I had three shot out from under me."

His Uncle Glen, who was about thirty, still robust and healthy looking, mumbled something like, "I'm glad to see you came through all right." He then took an intense interest in the soup he had just been served.

No other person, hostess or guest, spoke a word to him during the remainder of the meal, which, to Miss Emily anyway, he ate with too much gusto and way too many breaches of good etiquette. He used the wrong fork; used a short-handled spoon to stir his tea; slurped rather than sipped his wine. He noticed that he hadn't used the right spoon to stir his tea, but what th' heck the glass wasn't all that tall, anyway.

Just as everyone was picking up his or her dessert spoon, the butler came bustling in to whisper something in Miss Emily's ear. She immediately laid her spoon aside and rose to announce, "Good news, everybody! Evening Star is foaling in the south pasture!"

With cries of, "Let's go see the new colt," everybody got up from the table and bolted for the door—the men shucking their coats as they hurried across the veranda, the women gathering up their long, frilly skirts.

When the "stampede" had subsided, Ward sauntered out to the side lawn and then ambled on over to the gazebo near the far edge of the wide expanse of green. He stopped there to lean against a tree and watch as everyone disappeared down the long slope in the evening twilight.

Chapter 4

"You are not rushing down to witness the blessed event?"

Ward turned around and saw by the carriage shed light that it was Maggie Carson who had asked the teasing question.

He smiled, and drawled, "No, I grew up on a horse ranch in Texas where foaling was a regular thing that never drew half as big a crowd— most of th' time nobody at all.... What is so special about this perfectly natural horse-pasture event?"

"Well, you see," Maggie said, as she moved in a step closer, "this colt was sired by a prize-winning thoroughbred stallion at a famous breeding farm down in Kentucky. The Garrisons are quite sure it will grow up to be a super horse that will win every race it runs, and make the Garrison name world famous."

While Maggie was explaining the importance of the exciting event, she moved in another step. Close enough for Ward to see the curl of her lashes and the curve of her full red lips that remained so temptingly parted as she twiddled with a button on his jacket.

"So the Garrisons are gettin' into thoroughbred racing? Whose idea was that?" Ward asked.

"Why, Miss Emily's, of course," Maggie said, "I know you have been here less than a day, but can't you already see who's in charge around here?"

"Well, yes, I'm beginning to. How did she get to be the main ramrod?"

"Mister Andy willed everything to her."

"He did! Everything?"

"That's right. And every member of the Garrison family prospers in proportion to how well they please her. And even though they all try hard, none of them are prospering all that much—with the exception of Evan, Senior, and Evan, Junior. They seem to please her much more than the others."

"Hm-m-m," Ward said, "you don't often hear of a man willing everything to a second wife…didn't anybody challenge th' will?"

"Yes, Glen did. He hired a lawyer and took her to court. But he couldn't break it…and he is not back in her good graces yet, even though he works harder, for less, than any of the others."

"Well, how did Grandpa come to marry her, anyhow? I hear she came from way down in Tennessee."

"That's where she came from, all right. My mother says Mr. Andy first met her when he was down there on a horse buying trip about three months after your grandmother died.…Mister Andy hadn't been home a month before gold-digger Emily came to Marlin to visit a cousin who happened to be living here.

"With him being more than twice her age, Mom said it was shameful to see how she was throwing herself at Mister Andy. In two weeks' time she had him 'throwed and hog-tied' as you Texans might say…very much to my mother's bitter disappointment because she'd had her cap set for Mister Andy, too.

"When the knot was tied," Maggie went on as she continued to stand very close to Ward and twiddle with the buttons on his jacket, "Emily continued to cast her spell on Mister Andy. She sweet-talked him into selling the old home place downtown and build Garrison Manor. Which I hear is a copy, or nearly so, of the plantation home she claimed to have been brought up in down in Tennessee. They say she refused to stay a day in the old Garrison house in town, but lived in grand style in

a house Mister Andy rented for her until Garrison Manor was com-
pleted and furnished to her complete satisfaction.

"Anyway, my poor mother never got over losing out to Emily. To this
day she can't understand why Mister Andy chose Emily over her, since
at eighteen, to quote mother, she was much prettier than that 'Southern
wench from Tennessee'.

"She put up a brave front, though, and a few weeks later she married
my father who had just graduated from medical school. Judging from
what I've seen since I've become old enough to notice things, I don't
think my poor mother will ever get over it. She had another baby two
years after me but he was retarded. Probably because of the morphine
she was taking—and still takes from time to time when she is 'feeling
out of sorts'.

"Speaking of morphine, some folks think Emily got Mister Andy
hooked on it, and that's how she held such strong sway over him...get
him high on the stuff, and he'd do anything she wanted him to do. —
Like making out that new will just a few weeks before he died...that's
what some folks think, anyhow.

"Most folks think Mister Andy died of a heart attack, but my doctor
daddy said he had a strong heart. Some folks think he could have swallowed too many morphine pills by losing count, accidentally, or..."

"Or what," Ward urged her to go on.

"No, I don't want to say."

"Then let me guess...you were goin' t' say, 'or was urged to take',
weren't you?"

"I still don't want to say," Maggie shook her head. "After all you are
family and I don't want to offend." She lifted her eyes beseechingly, bid-
ding for assurance that she hadn't already said too much.

"Well," Ward said, "isn't Evan, Junior about to make you a part of the
family?"

"Well, maybe," Maggie looked away, "he has given me a ring, but I still haven't worn it...I don't know if I ever will. I can't get him to warm up and show the passions that a serious suitor should..."

Ward certainly couldn't imagine why, because his passions were already aroused way beyond what was proper between two soon-to-be cousins.

When she pushed him way beyond his power to resist by leaning against him, he crushed her yielding body against his and kissed her waiting lips.

In passion's giddyland he swept her up in his arms, and through a lilac-scented lavender haze he carried her to the carriage shed and laid her on the seat of the biggest, plushest carriage of them all. She quickly positioned herself on the velvet cushions, drew her dress up, and started removing her panties.

With the last of his restraint totally gone, Ward's passion matched Maggie's, and two lovers never gave more of themselves and been so exhausted after climax!

As they lay in each other's arms, their senses dulled with lingering passion, they didn't hear the footsteps or see the light from the lanterns. They were totally unaware of anyone's presence up to the very moment when Ward was so rudely yanked from the carriage by his heels!

He managed to land on his feet but his pants were still down around his knees. He reached for them with one hand while he tried to fend Evan, Jr. off with the other. He took a solid clout to his jaw, but before his outraged cousin could land another blow he shoved him back into a hedge and that gave him time to pull his pants up.

He had never been so embarrassed in his life. But it was no time for penitence and self-reproach...he had to defend himself against a mad-as-hell suitor.

Actually he didn't want to fight Evan. After all, he was blood kin and not nearly as big and strong as he was. So instead of pummeling him around in front of everybody, he ducked a wild swing, spun him around and clamped his arms around him from behind.

But his outraged cousin wouldn't stop struggling until his Uncle Glen stepped up, and said, "All right, that's enough! Stop it!"

Two other Garrisons stepped in at that point, and with more roughness than was needed, jerked Ward back and shoved him up against the carriage. When his manhandling cousins finally let him go, he immediately made a move to leave but he found Miss Emily blocking in his way.

"Yankee scum!" she spat the words at him like an angry cat, "I should have known better than invite the likes of you into my house. How dare you insult the whole Garrison family with your low-life, barnyard behavior? Get off these premises at once, and don't you ever come back!"

"Don't worry about it, Ma'am," Ward said, with a steely look in his eye, "I wouldn't think of dishonoring the memory of the good men who fell beside me, by ever again setting foot on this treasonous ground!"

While Miss Emily was swooning dead away in Evan, Sr.'s arms, Ward stalked around the carriage shed to where he had left his horse, mounted up and rode away without a backward look. But he couldn't help wondering what would happen to Maggie? He felt bad about leaving her behind to face everyone's wrath.

Chapter 5

Back in his room, stretched out on the bed, Ward tried to get some control of his troubling thoughts....He didn't feel the least bit proud of himself, letting Maggie seduce him like that. And then, while he was still in his lavender haze, letting them get caught in such a compromising way.

He couldn't blame Evan, Jr. for being so outraged and coming at him like he had. And he honestly couldn't blame Miss Emily for being angry with him. But she had gone way too far in calling him "Yankee scum" and he was not sorry for what he said back to her.

He damn well resented her Southern airs and her obvious sympathy for the South. He finally figured it out....She wasn't wearing black because President Lincoln had been assassinated. It was out of her bitter grief for the defeated Confederacy and the legitimacy it had given to slavery and the high-falutin way of life it supported.

He wondered what his daddy was going to say when he heard about it all. He'd have to tell him everything when he got home...why he and Evan had fought, and about Miss Emily ordering him off her premises. When he'd heard it all he would without doubt fall on the floor and laugh so hard he'd give himself a hernia! Especially when he heard the part about him and Maggie being caught with their behinds looming like two full moons rising over the prairie!

But then, when he was able to get back on his feet, he'd probably say, "I'm proud of you, Son. I'm glad you told the arrogant bitch off. And I'm glad you let the whole bunch know that you resented the way the men had all stayed home making themselves rich, while you fought through four years of hell savin' th' country for them and everybody else."

And he might go on to say, "Forgive me for not telling you about Emily. I didn't think any of us would ever go back for a visit and I wanted all of my kids to grow up thinking they had a real live grandmother." (Ward remembered that his grandparents on his mother's side had died in an epidemic soon after she was born, leaving her to be raised by an aunt.)

While still feeling like an interloper who should have never even thought about stopping by Marlin for a family visit, he was about to drop off to sleep when he heard a soft knock on the door. He immediately got out of bed to go see who it could be. As he was reaching for the knob he spotted a white envelope that had been slipped under the door. He picked it up and immediately opened the door but there was no one there.

He lit a lamp, opened the envelope, unfolded the sheet of paper, and read: "My man will have already left a horse downstairs for you. Please get on it and ride out of town tonight! Your life is no longer safe around Marlin!…'Buck' and the saddle are yours to keep." The note was signed: Glen Garrison.

So Evan, in his mounting rage, was finding it impossible to reconcile himself to his and Maggie's thoughtless 'indiscretion'. His egotistical cousin couldn't understand her finding it easy to forget him while she found the pleasure he wouldn't give her in some other man's arms. He could have headed the whole thing off by showing more "interest" in Maggie, instead of slaving his life away on boring business matters.

He felt sorry for Maggie and guilty for the way he had run out on her. But then he got the feeling that Maggie would land on her feet like a cat.

Anyway, there was no help for any of it now. The fat was already in the fire and he agreed with his Uncle Glen.…He should nip the whole affair in the bud and without causing anymore embarrassment, grab his duffel bag and get his butt out of town. He sure didn't want to get himself shot by a jealous cousin, and he hated the thought of shooting Evan nearly as much…and what th' heck, he'd be leaving town only a few hours ahead of when he'd been aiming to, anyhow.

*   *   *

When he had ridden four or five miles down the road toward Cairo, he figured—if Evan was coming after him—that that would be farther than it would take for his tender butt to persuade his bruised ego to give up the chase. He'd chance it because it had been a long, exhausting, emotion-draining day and he was tired. He had fought through daylong battles that hadn't left him half so fagged out.

When he was sure he couldn't hear riders on the trail behind him, he rode into the edge of a meadow behind a grove of trees. He tethered the horse his Uncle Glen had so kindly provided, spread his blanket on the lush spring grass, and laid himself down for some much-needed sleep.

At sunrise he was still in deep sleep, and would have gone on snoozing for another hour if "Buck" hadn't nickered. He soon heard what the keen-eared horse had already heard…at least two riders coming at a fast clip down the road from Marlin.

He got to his feet, rubbed the sleep out of his eyes and shifted his old horse pistol around to the front of his waist band where it would be easier to get at. He didn't really expect one of the riders to be Evan, but he knew that highway robbers were taking advantage of the chaotic times, and were prowling lonely stretches of road looking for easy prey.

He didn't recognize either of the riders as they came at a fast canter through some still dark shadows in the early morning mist. But then as they rode through a broad shaft of sunlight, he saw that one of them was indeed Evan. He immediately stepped into the road ready to draw and start firing. If his hotheaded cousin wanted a fight bad enough to ride half the night to catch up with him, he reckoned he'd have to accommodate him.

But Evan reined his horse in, raised his hand, and said, "No that's not the way we'll do it. We'll do it like gentlemen, and this is just the right time of day for it."

He dismounted and then went on to say, "I'm talking about a gentleman's duel.…We'll stand back-to-back and each of us will then take five steps as my second counts them off. When he gets to five, we'll both turn and fire."

"All right," Ward said, "if you won't have it any other way. But first let me say this.…It wasn't Maggie's fault. She sipped a little too much wine and I took advantage.…I apologize to you and her. And since I've already left town with my tail between my legs, that ought to give you enough satisfaction. I sure don't think one of us has t' be killed to settle this matter. I don't see it as being something you can't live with, since we probably won't ever see each other again."

"I disagree," the proud fool refused to be mollified, "it's a matter of honor, and since I'm the offended party I demand satisfaction. What's more I get to choose the weapons…I therefore choose pistols to be used as I've just described…so let's move the horses out of the line of fire and get on with it."

Evan's cool demeanor and the way he seemed to be so detached, puzzled Ward. He was not acting like a man who was about to fight for his life, but more like some director staging a play in which he was also going to be playing one of the main parts.

He remembered one of his troopers who was going into battle acting a lot like Evan was acting. He later learned that the trooper had just downed two gulps of laudanum from a bottle he'd stolen from an aid station. Had Evan downed some of that opium concoction? Or had he popped a couple of morphine pills? No matter, he'd still be looking over the sights of a loaded pistol, and such drugs don't render one entirely blind.

"All right," Evan almost shouted, his voice pitched high, his eyes wide and bright, "pistols at the ready, contestants back-to-back...second, start counting!"

"One, two, three, four..."

At the count of four Ward heard Evan's shot and felt the bullet nick his right ear as it whizzed past his head!

What a too-trusting fool he was! And that was no single-shot, old-fashioned dueling pistol Evan had in his hand...there were five more shots in that thing!

He ducked into a crouch and swung around with his pistol leveled. His dishonorable cousin was standing sidewise in the traditional dueling stance and was taking aim for another shot at his head! But Ward's bullet plowed through his fat buttocks and threw his aim off.

Evan collapsed on the ground and started yelling to his second, "Kill him! Kill him!"

But his second was already looking into the muzzle of Ward's old horse pistol. So instead of foolishly trying to obey Evan's ignoble command he wisely dropped his pistol and lifted his hands. While his dishonorable cousin was holding his bloody buttocks and writhing in pain, Ward picked up their guns and threw them deep into the woods.

"Now," he said to Evan's lackey, "get your boss on his horse—I think he'd prefer to be belly down—and get th' hell outa here before I decide to give both of you treacherous bastards what you deserve."

Chapter 6

As Ward was putting his old pistol back in its holster, he couldn't help smiling at the picture that came to his mind…his arrogant cousin ridin' into town belly down across his saddle, with his bloody behind on public display! It was good enough for the pompous, dishonorable bastard. It might bring him down to earth, teach him a little humility and make him realize that he wasn't such a high and mighty Lord of the Manor, after all.

He wagged his head as he fastened the flap on his old muzzle-loader. As much as he was wishing it hadn't happened, here was another shameful family story he'd have to tell his daddy. But to lessen the chance of causing him to overstrain himself, he'd space his stories out and not tell them all at the first sitting.

He rolled up his blanket, saddled ol' Buck and got back on the long trail to Brushy Creek. He could hardly believe that the family visit he had looked forward to with so many pleasant thoughts had turned out to be such a terrible disappointment—not to mention his near-murder at the hands of a treacherous cousin!

He remembered—with an ironic smile—that he had planned, if the right moment had come along, to ask his grandmother for a loan to help him get his cattle ranch started. The certainty of a good inheritance would've stood good for it.

What a jackass laugh that had turned out to be! Grandfather Andy's fortune would now wind up in the hands of Emily's kin...Southern Rebels if you please! What a kick in the pants that would be for the Garrisons, especially a starry-eyed Texas boy who had come "to help his Illinois kinfolk fight off those hordes of Southern Rebels!"

But what the hell, he was glad he had helped save the Union and free the slaves, and he could get along without any loan or inheritance. He was alive, still young and strong and had survived a score of bloody battles. Death had passed him by a hundred times, the last time less than an hour ago...surely for some good purpose.

He squared his shoulders, urged Buck into a long-striding canter, and bared his teeth to the wind with a big Texas smile. There was still a lot of life to be lived, girls to be loved, and a ranch to be started with a thousand longhorns waiting to be rounded up!

Some three hours and fifteen miles later his stomach reminded him that he'd had no breakfast and it was nearly noon. He knew it couldn't be much farther to Cairo—if he hadn't taken the wrong fork in the road two miles back? He was beginning to wonder if he should turn back and take the other fork, when he spotted a sign in the high weeds that informed hungry travelers that "Clancy's Inn" was only one mile ahead.

"Come on, Buck," he urged, "I'm sure we'll find some chow there for you, too."

Responding as if he had understood his new master's words, the equally hungry steed found the energy to cover the long mile in less than three minutes.

As soon as they arrived at Clancy's Inn on the outskirts of Cairo, Ward showed Buck his appreciation by seeing that he was watered, rubbed down, and got his chow first.

His Uncle Glen had certainly not given him some winded old nag he was about to ship off to some glue factory. He had given him a blooded charger with speed and stamina....Maybe he had figured his "intemperate" Texas nephew would need a fast horse to outpace Evan on one of his prize steeds. Anyway, he was grateful and would always have a warm spot in his heart for his Uncle Glen. He wondered how his thoughtful uncle would take it when he found out that he had shot Evan in his big fat behind!

On a side porch at Clancy's Inn he found a big washstand that was fully equipped with wash pan, water bucket, homemade soap, and a cracked mirror. There was also a towel that had already been used by too many grimy travelers who hadn't used enough soap.

Ward hung his hat on a nail, rolled his sleeves up, poured a pan full of water and reached for the hunk of ominous-looking soap. His wash-up made him feel better except for the soap that was stinging his eyes so much he couldn't see. He started groping all around for the towel, but he couldn't put a hand on it....Damn it, he had seen it hanging right there on a nail just a minute ago...

"Here's a towel...I brought you a clean one."

It was the voice from a thousand dreams...a voice he'd been yearning to hear ever since he'd figured out that every man had to have a just-right woman to fill the empty void his life. His eyes flew open, but his vision was so blurred by the soap he couldn't clearly see the girl with the voice he'd heard in his dreams.

The blurry vision said, "Here, I'll help you...I've been telling Mother she makes the soap too strong."

Her melodious words started Ward's whole being to vibrating again like a big tuning fork. He tried to open his eyes to see the dream that had come true, but the dream pressed the towel against them, and said, "No, don't try to open them. Wait for some tears to wash that soap out."

Finally the dream removed the towel from his eyes and let it fall into his hands. He blinked to clear the last of the soap out of his eyes and finally got them focused.

Her voice had indeed struck a resonating chord, but the sight of her smiling face sent a whole wave of chords from the top of his head to the tips of his toes. But for all of the wondrous resonating chords he was feeling in every other part of his body, his vocal chords were paralyzed. He couldn't utter a word. His mouth and tongue were working but not a syllable came out.

"Now let me guess," his dream-come-true said, as she looked him up and down, "you are on your way back home to Texas, after fighting on the Union side. That has to mean your folks were originally from the North…you wouldn't be having kin here in Southern Illinois, would you?"

Ward's mouth had stopped gaping like a minnow's in a dried up stock pond, but he still couldn't stop staring at her. She was the girl of his dreams all right…eyes as blue as the sky after an April shower…cheeks as pink as a prairie primrose…

Her pert nose was two notches above perfection, and her lips were as red as a a ripe cherry. But that wasn't all, her high-necked dress and the bib of her apron didn't come close to hiding all of the curves of her shapely breasts and shoulders.

Finally, after giving his face and hands a last wipe with the towel, he was able to say, "You are a good guesser. I **am** from Texas and I did fight on the Union side. But since I'm wearing Yankee blue, I can't give you an 'A' for that.

"But I'll have to give you a high mark for guessing that I have some kin around here.…My name is Ward Garrison, and I'm kin to the Garrisons who live up in Marlin. But I'd just as soon you didn't go around tellin' everybody, because I have just found out some things that don't make me especially proud to claim the relationship."

His dream gave him a one-shouldered shrug, and said, "If that's the way you want it.…My name is Thomasina McGee," she went on to tell him as her smile faded just a bit, "they call me Sina for short."

She then came back with a brighter look, and said, "Would you look at me?…Standing here prattling my head off while you are starving! Come on in.…My mother makes the best Irish stew this side of the old Emerald Isle, itself."

She led Ward to a handsome home-crafted table with chairs to match, and then went on to the kitchen. Because he was a man, she was quite sure that he was following her with his eyes....She tried her best to keep her hips from swinging.

She was right. Ward had kept his eyes on her all the way to the kitchen door. And the sight of her hips, along with her exquisitely sculpted ankles and calves, left him with an ache in his throat.

She couldn't be married...Lord don't let it be so. She hadn't acted like a married woman...being so friendly.

He of course didn't know that she had seen him ride in, had watched him around the barn, and had offered up the very same prayer regarding his marital status.

Ward's eyes were still glued to the kitchen door when Sina reappeared with a loaded tray. She set the tray of vittles on the table within easy reach of her hungry patron and turned to leave. But as she was turning away, Ward put out his hand and said, "If...if you are not too busy, would you just sit a minute so we can talk?"

Sina almost blurted out, "I was scared to death you weren't going to ask!" But instead of being so forward, she smiled agreeably, and said, "Of course. I'd love to."

When she was seated across from him, Ward said, "Out there a minute ago when I told you I was a Garrison, your face kinda fell and you looked away. Is it all that bad...me bein' a Garrison?"

"No, of course not," she assured him, "having grown up in Texas you are not really one of them. You can't help what they've done, or haven't done."

"You mean like hiring substitutes to go do their fightin'?"

"Well, yes-s...but don't ask me to go on talking about them because, after all, they are still your kin folks."

"What if I told you that I shot one of my cousins this morning?"

"What! Why did you shoot him? I hope you didn't kill him!"

"No, I didn't kill him," Ward assured her, "but he won't be sittin' down to any of his meals for a few days."

Sina gasped, and then with a twinkle in her eye, she said, "You mean you shot him in the seat of his pants? An ex-cavalry officer couldn't be that bad a shot...I'm betting you did it on purpose."

"Yeah...standin' sidewise like he was in his Southern-style dueling stance, his behind presented such a big, invitin' target."

"That nick on your right ear...I'll bet he got off the first shot while your back was still turned," she correctly guessed.

"Yeah, that's what happened," Ward admitted, "I can be awfully stupid sometimes."

Sina breathed a prayer of thanks, and said, "Not stupid...just too trusting. But you can't go on believing that everybody holds to the same high standards as you do. I'm sure glad I learned that fact early in my life."

Ward looked at her and wondered about what she had said. He finally decided she was just referring to the age-old problem young girls have of learning to fend off predatory men.

"By the way," Sina went on, "you still haven't told me why you and your cousin were fighting."

When Ward hung his head and wouldn't meet her eye, she smiled, and said, "Never mind. I'm sure I can guess that, too. I've heard about Maggie Carson and how she can't resist a handsome man."

With a sheepish grin, Ward said, "You have guessed right. But I am not entirely blameless. —Now," he quickly continued, "I've told you my story about the draft-dodgin' Garrisons, and I've got th' feelin' you have one you could tell me....So how about it?...I'd like to hear some more about my rich, but maybe not so honorable kin folks."

"All right," Sina said, a little hesitantly, "here's one that goes way back and had some effect on my life...maybe you won't be too offended by it...

"Once upon a time my mother's parents ran a small hotel up in Marlin. But when mother was just seventeen both of her parents died in a typhoid epidemic, leaving her and an old black couple to run the hotel—with the added burden of raising two young brothers.

"Well, to everyone's surprise the young Quaker girl and the old black couple did quite well—both at running the hotel and raising the boys. Then when the hard working orphan girl had blossomed into a very attractive woman with a thriving business, guess who became her most frequent caller and the most persistent petitioner for her hand? —Evan Garrison! That would be Evan Senior, Evan Junior's pa. But much to Evan's consternation she kept on putting him off.

"Then one day along comes this young Irish charmer named Clancy McGee, and without a dime in his pocket he checks into Mother's hotel. After two days she asked Clancy if he intended to pay by the day or by the week.

"'Sure and I'll be payin' you by the minute if you have some work I can do,' he replied. Whereupon she handed him a broom and a dustpan and pointed to the stairs.

"Clancy soon proved that he wasn't afraid of work. In a short time he became the hotel's night clerk, house detective and general handyman. —And a more and more frequent date for its proprietor.

"At the end of the first month, when they sat down to settle up, Clancy said, 'Sure and I do believe Mary, Darlin', it would be less time and bother if we just got married and dispensed with all of this time-keepin' and calculatin'.'

"Mother laughed and said she thought it was a good idea, too. So they got married and soon became everybody's favorite couple...**everybody's except the Garrison's.** But even without the Garrison's good will, the young couple thrived for two good years. But then, just after I was born, they were forced to give up the hotel.

"That's right. After twenty years the Albright Hotel was forced to close its doors. I can see you have already guessed, but let me fill in a detail or two...

"Miss Emily, the new Mrs. Andrew Garrison, was already taking a strong hand in Garrison business affairs. And upon Evan's spiteful request she persuaded Mister Andy to buy the building the hotel was in, put the McGees out, and let her no-good cousin move in to run it.

"Well, fortunately, the frugal Quaker girl and her Scotch-Irish husband had squirreled away some money. They bought a couple of acres here and built this inn—most of it with their own hands."

While Sina had been talking, Ward had been hanging on to her every word. Not just because he was hearing another shocking story of the Garrison family's imperious behavior, but because of the way her lips moved, and the way the dimples in her cheeks darted in and out.

A time or two under his adoring gaze, Sina had dropped her eyes and blushed. She had never met a man who was so unafraid of showing his deepest feelings the way Ward was showing his...no effort to hide or guard them lest he be hurt by heartless rejection.

There'd be no rejection from her, but she knew she had to show some restraint. A proper Quaker girl couldn't go falling head over heels in love with a man after an acquaintance of less than two hours!

Finally Ward said, "I wish I could turn th' calendar back and maybe do something about the raw deal your parents suffered at Garrison hands. But of course I can't. By the way," he went on, "I caught a glimpse of your mother awhile ago and I must say she is still quite a looker. But I'm wonderin' about your Irish daddy. Where is he? I'd like to meet him."

Tears welled up in Sina's eyes and her lips trembled. "He's dead," she said, barely above a whisper, "about a year ago."

She dabbed at her eyes and went on to say, "With all of his lovable qualities, Daddy had one little flaw...he loved to go carousing in barrooms. Not every night, mind you, but like once a month. Mother used to laugh and say the full moon had something to do with it. But she never nagged him about it. She knew it was as much a part of him as his charming Irish brogue.

"Every time as he was about to leave on one of his carousing nights, Mother would say, 'Clancy, try not to get mixed up in another brawl and come home with your good shirt torn and your nose all bloody'. To which he'd always reply, 'I won't, Mary, Darlin'. I'm just goin' t' have a mug of grog, toss a few darts, and come straight home'…he always promised, but he never did.

"Well, one night, much later than usual, he just barely dragged himself home. This time it was his shirt that was bloody. Bloody from a deep stab wound in his side. He died out there on the steps in Mother's arms…

"Back when the war began, some folks around Cairo had started showing their true colors. Some of them quite openly sided with the South. Well, my Irish Daddy never failed to let them know how he felt about the slave-holding South and its sympathizers. On this particular night Clancy had started another brawl, but the barkeep said Clancy was still unblooded when he left the saloon.

"Somebody had waylaid him and stabbed him on his way home. But the only clue we have is a name that he mumbled before he died. The name he mumbled sounded like 'Murphy'. But nobody knew a Murphy who'd been involved in the brawl…

"I can't believe th' way I'm carryin' on," Sina scolded herself, "like my whole life has been nothin' but one tragedy after another. It certainly hasn't," she said, as a smile came back to her face, "I've had some fun and I've had the privilege of doing some things that have given me an awful lot of satisfaction."

"Well," Ward said, as he spooned out the last tidbit of stew, "go ahead, tell me about some of them."

"Not now," Sina laughed, "I have a feeling you'd like to rest up a bit, and then have yourself a look-see around Cairo. As for me, I've got work waiting for me in the kitchen."

When Ward had stopped at Clancy's Inn he'd had no intention of staying the night, but he smiled in agreement, signed the register, and went to take a bath and a much-needed nap.

Chapter 7

Ward found the saloon that Sina had recommended....She had told him that most poker hands were dealt straight in the BRASS RAI L...

He pushed his way through the swinging doors and spotted a table in a far corner with only four players. When he flashed a good-sized roll of Yankee greenbacks they all "licked their chops" and nodded their approval for him to join in and start "donating".

As he was bringing up a chair and getting himself seated, he looked around the table to size up his opponents. One of the four was no doubt a riverboat man...a first mate, maybe a captain. The second one was most likely a store clerk. The third player looked like a mill hand. The fourth one had to be a horse trader on his way to or from Kentucky. They all looked fairly honest...

He was surprised when he won the first hand. He was even more surprised when he won three out of the first five. But then his luck tailed off. He lost all he had won and was about to quit the game when he started winning again.

He won two straight hands and raked in two big pots. He folded on the next hand, but on the next one he decided to stay with two pair—deuces and tens. All of the other players stayed, with two of them raising. Ward didn't do any raising, he just called and stayed in for the draw.

Everybody took three cards except Ward and the horse trader. They each took one. The opener, who was sitting to Ward's right, bet a modest amount…probably hadn't got any help.

Ward's luck had stayed with him. He had drawn a third ten to give him a full house. He quite properly raised by a goodly amount. —He didn't want to be accused of sucking everybody in to sweeten the pot. The two players ahead of the horse trader just called, but the dobbin dealer immediately raised Ward's bet.

The nag merchant had stayed with a pair of aces and a pair of kings. He had drawn no help but since one of the aces he was holding was the spade ace he knew that no two pair could beat him. From his reading of the cards that he'd been slyly marking, he was sure that Ward had gone in with two pair, had got no help, and was bluffing…counting on everybody remembering the good hands he'd been getting.

The opener immediately folded, but Ward raised the horse trader right back. The other players folded and left it up to the nag dealer. He quite confidently shoved out another big raise. Ward saw his raise and doubled it.

The horse dealer emptied his pockets but came up short.

"I can cover only a part of your raise," he said.

"Well, let's see," Ward said, "you are about thirty dollars short. How about that gun and holster you are packing? You can cover the rest of my bet with them."

The horse trader readily agreed. And while he grinned like a city slicker fleecing at a backwoods hick, he shucked off the belt with its holstered gun and laid it on the pile of bills in the middle of the table. He knew he'd be getting his new six-shooter back in just a moment, along with the biggest pot of the night.

He laid out his aces and kings and was reaching for the pot, when Ward spread his full house. As Ward pulled in the big pot the horse trader turned as gray as a tombstone and looked as if he might lose his supper…he had misread one of his amateurish markings.

Ward slipped the gun from its holster and saw that it was exactly what he had thought it was...a new Colt .45 that fired factory made shells.

"I'll buy any forty-five shells you may have," Ward offered.

"I have two boxes," the dobbin dealer replied, "but they'll cost you five dollars a box," which was twice what he had paid for them. Ward handed him ten dollars and the crestfallen card marker handed over the two boxes of shells. Ward didn't mind paying the big loser the double price.

The ex-captain of cavalry was strapping on his newly won six-shooter, when a wharf rat wearing a tattered cap and an old bosun's coat moved in close to urgently whisper in his ear, "There are two men coming after you. I'm sure they aim to kill you!...Come on, we can go out the back door."

She had fooled his eyes but she couldn't change her voice enough to fool him into thinking she was a man. The "wharf rat" was Sina.

"What are you doing here?" Ward asked, still a little giddy over his winnings, especially the new Colt .45.

"I told you," Sina hissed, "two men are on their way here to kill you. We have to get out of here, now!"

"Well, now," Ward was slow to be stampeded, "let's don't rush out and maybe run into an ambush...you just stay out of th' way and let me handle them."

The saloon doors suddenly swung back and two hulking brutes with pistols in their belts swaggered into the room.

"That's them!" Sina hissed, as one of the brutes moved to the right, while the other one was moving two steps to the left. With them presenting two widely separated targets Ward hoped he'd have time to get off a second shot.

After another quick look he recognized the one on the left as having been Evan's "second" at the phony duel in which he came close to being shot in the back of his head. He had never seen the thuggish-looking man that was standing well to the right, but he had seen his type. —A killer whose deadly profession was for sale to any dishonorable person who could afford the service he offered…Ward knew he'd have to get him first.

"All right, mister," Evan's lackey said, "we've come to take you back to Marlin to stand trial for attempted murder."

"Then I suppose you have a badge you can show, and a warrant," Ward challenged, "but even if you do," he went on, "I'm sure you are out of your jurisdiction."

Evan's man-Friday looked over at his kill-for-pay partner, and said, "Well, Murphy, I guess we'll just have to do it the hard way!"

A satanic grin split the mad killer's bearded face.…The easy five hundred he was about to earn would set him up in Chicago for another month of wild debauchery. With a bloodcurdling yell that was supposed to unnerve his prey, he reached for the gun in his belt.

But Ward had heard too many bloodcurdling rebel yells to be intimidated.…The big Colt slid smoothly from its holster and its powerful blast rocked the room. The big slug it launched with its blast slammed the killer back against the wall. As he was slumping to the floor the bloodcurdling yell that was supposed to paralyze his prey ended in a whimpery little gurgle.

Ward thumbed the big Colt's hammer and was hoping he could bring the muzzle on target before he caught a slug in his own gut. But as he was bringing the muzzle to bear he saw that the treacherous lackey's knees were already buckling!

He glanced to his left and saw smoke curling from the muzzle of the little derringer in Sina's hand. It's little "pop-gun" report had been drowned out by the blast of his big .45. He gave her a nod of thanks for backing him up.

With their guns still in hand they moved up to where the two would-be killers were sprawled on the floor. They saw that Evan's hireling was still alive and conscious. Ward rolled him over with his foot and while he stared down at him, he asked, "Did Evan hire you two to kill me?"

The downed lackey moved his head from side-to-side, and said, "Not Evan…Miss Emily."

Ward looked at Sina and she said, "I'm not at all surprised."

She then looked down at the one Ward had shot, and asked, "Did you hear what he called this one?"

Ward said, "Yeah, let's see if he can still talk."

The barkeeper, who had already turned the killer-for-hire over on his back, looked up at them, and said, "He won't be telling you anything."

Sina saw the wicked-looking knife that had slipped from his scabbard when the barkeep turned him over…

"Do you remember the last night my Daddy was in here, and was then killed on his way home?" she asked the barkeep, "can you remember seeing this one in here that night?"

The barkeeper—who had finally recognized Sina—looked at the bearded brute from one side then the other, and finally said, "He looks familiar. I'm sure I've seen him before…maybe when he didn't have a beard, just a moustache…yeah, I'm sure he was in here that night."

At that point the town doctor came in, followed by a policeman. The old doctor glanced at the killer sprawled on the floor with blood oozing from just below his wishbone.

"There is nothing I can do for him," he declared, "but let's see about this one. Ah," he went on as he knelt beside Evan's erstwhile lackey, "small caliber bullet with a light load behind it. I don't think this one is hurt very bad. With the bullet extracted and a tight bandage, he'll be up and around in no time."

When everybody had assured the policeman that it was self-defense, he nodded his head and indicated that Ward and the "wharf rat" could go ahead and leave.

When they were outside, Ward asked Sina, "How did you know they were after me?"

"They asked about you at the Inn," Sina replied. "Mother told them she hadn't seen you but they forced her to hand over the register. You should feel honored…it's a rare thing for a Quaker to tell a lie.

"When they went upstairs to look for you, I ran outside, untied their horses, hazed one of them away and rode the other one here. Thank Heaven I got here with some time to spare," she went on with a penitent little smile, "because I had to break into a second-hand store and 'borrow' these clothes. It's right around the corner…I'll take them off and put them back. Being a woman, I had to disguise myself to get in the saloon."

As they were about to mount up, Ward said, "The one Evan's lackey called Murphy, do you think he may have been the one who stabbed Clancy?"

As she remembered with both anger and sadness, Sina said, "Well, you saw the knife, and the barkeep said he was sure he'd been in there."

"Then we probably settled a score for your daddy. Do you think somebody could have paid the killer to do it?"

"Yes, I think he was paid. And I'm sure we can now guess who paid him."

"Yeah," Ward grunted, "and that reminds me, I now have a score of my own to settle with her…sendin' those two jaspers after me like that."

"Ward," Sina said, "you have a score besides that one to settle with Miss Emily. But I don't want to talk about her anymore tonight. Let's just be thankful we are both still alive and well."

"All right," Ward agreed, "but I want to say thanks for your help…I'm not sure I could've got off a second shot soon enough. You showed a lot of spunk…comin' to warn me and then backin' me up like that.…You are a woman any man would be proud t' take to Texas!"

Sina laughed, and said, "Well, now, Mr. Tall Handsome Texan, if that is a proposal I'll think it over.…But for now, lets get these clothes back in that store and get on home so Mother can get off her knees and see that her prayer has been answered!"

Chapter 8

The next morning as they were having a late breakfast, Sina laid her fork down, and said, "Back to what we said last night about us both having scores to settle with Miss Emily, it's more than that, now…

"It came to me last night.…We now have to protect Jo."

"Jo?" Ward said, "th' girl that works in your kitchen? Why does she need protectin'?"

"Well, let me start by telling you a little story. She was one of a group of slaves that Clancy and I helped to escape across the river two years ago. We hid them in the barn for a few days so they could rest and change into some other clothes…"

"Why did you have to hide them?" Ward broke in to ask, "after they got across the Ohio into Illinois, weren't they free to go and come as they pleased?"

"No," Sina said, "not here in Southern Illinois. There were too many greedy bounty hunters looking for escaped slaves to catch and return to their masters for the bounties they offered…

"After three days," she went on, "Jo and the others were anxious to move on north where they could really be free and get work. The day they left we packed them some food and gave them some money, and as they were leaving we reminded them again to be sure to go around Marlin.

"But, unfortunately, they got on a road that was being watched by two bounty-hunting deputies and they were pounced on. And as usual, the bounty hunters loaded them in their wagons and took them to the Garrison Manor to let Miss Emily have her pick of the lot. She added Jo and another girl to her staff of "servants"…she calls them servants but for all the freedom she allows them, they are the same as her slaves.

"A week ago when Jo heard that the war was finally over and all slaves had been freed, she escaped and came here to hide. She is scared to death that Miss Emily will find out where she is, and to keep her from telling some things that she heard the older servants whispering about she will have her killed."

"You mean she may have heard them whisperin' about what Miss Emily did to my grandfather?" Ward asked with a glint in his eye.

"Yes, about how she was always urging him to take more morphine, and finally forced him to take a fatal dose."

"Then Maggie was tellin' it right," Ward remembered, "so what do you think?… What can we do to keep Emily from finding out she is here?""

"I'm afraid it's too late for that," Sina said, "I'm sure that Evan's lackey saw Jo last night and recognized her. And since he wasn't hurt too bad by my shot, we have to assume that he has already dispatched someone with a note to Miss Emily, telling her that he saw Jo and where he saw her. She will no doubt send someone to her brother with an urgent request for him to come at once. Jo knows about Emily's brother and that's why she's so scared…

"Emily's brother is a killer…not just a crazy, penny-ante killer like the one you shot last night, but a killer with a cause.… He is crafty, insidious, and has made assassination an art. He was—probably still is—a Confederate agent, and was a thorn in the side of the Union Army all through the war…spying on them, assassinating important officials, and killing several of their best secret agents.

"They tried desperately to find him so they could hang him. I'm sure they still are, but he has too many southern supporters and too many places to hide. Besides that, I hear that he is very clever at disguising himself and changing his whole appearance. Not that it will help us much, but his real name is Gideon P. Haliburton.

"I'm sure Emily knows where to send her courier—probably somewhere in Kentucky where he has romantic interests, and where he likes to hide out between missions. A courier could already be on his way to him with Emily's note. In another two or three days he could be sitting right over there waiting for a chance to kill Jo!

"Ward, we have to get ready to stop him. Not just because we care for Jo, but because she can help us expose Emily for what she is. With the killer she fears out of the way, I'm sure Jo will tell the District Attorney everything she has heard.... After he has brought in some of the older 'servants' to verify her story, he can then have Mister Andy's body exhumed for positive proof, and Miss Emily will be on her way to prison."

"Yeah," Ward nodded his head, "I'm all for that. And from what you say, that brother of hers is long overdue for a big dose of Justice, himself...

"As far as us gettin' ready for him, I'm thinkin' he'll be comin' by way of the Kentucky-Cairo ferry, and since we don't want him to get any where near Jo, don't you think th' best place to stop him would be at th' ferry landing?"

Sina nodded her head and said, "Jo has seen Gideon and can give you a description..."

Ward went on to say, "OK, so I'll start hangin' around th' landin' **tomorrow to get familiar with th' lay of th' land. And I'll get myself ready to stop any suspicious lookin' jasper that comes down th' gang**-plank.... But on th' chance that he might come by a different route, you have t' start bein' careful about servin' any stranger that comes in, and see that Jo stays out of sight."

Sina agreed and acknowledged his instructions. Then, with a grave look on her face, she put her hand on Ward's arm, and said, "Ward, please don't take any foolish chances with this man like you did with Evan. From what I've heard he is a man totally without conscience... a man who still considers himself an agent of the Confederacy with a license to kill anyone who contributed to its defeat!"

Ward took her hand, and said, "I'll be careful, 'cause I want to have a long, happy life with you."

Chapter 9

Jo had gotten only a brief glimpse of Gideon one day during the war when he was hiding out at the Garrison Manor. According to her best description he was a medium sized white man in his thirties, and at the time she saw him, his hair was dark and hung nearly to his shoulders. It was not much to go on, but she had noticed one thing that might be of some help, his eyebrows and eyelashes had been almost white.

From the timetable Ward had calculated, it would take the killer at least three days to get to Cairo. But on the third day no man matching Jo's skimpy description got off the ferry at the end of any of its three trips to the Kentucky shore and back. He hadn't really expected to see one that soon, but the scrutinizing he'd given every man that came down the gangplank had been good practice. It was the same thing again the next day…no likely looking killer to start his palms sweating and his pulse to pounding.

On the fifth day he began to wonder if the crafty killer had somehow been alerted that the Cairo ferry was being watched, and had warily chosen to come by some other route. But he didn't let the thought diminish his vigilance…he'd at least stay alert and keep a sharp watch…

To keep himself more alert he started trying to relate every man who came down the gangplank to a line of work: Was he a salesman, a doctor, a lawyer, a farmer, a lumberjack, a shoemaker, or a cold-blooded assassin?

The first one off the boat when it docked just after noon was easy. The feller wearing the soiled frock coat and carrying the medicine bag, was obviously a doctor or a veterinarian returning from a house call on the Kentucky side. Besides him looking like a vet or a doctor, he was too old to be Gideon.

The short, bearded fellow struggling with the big backpack had to be an old Jewish peddler, back from hawking his sewing notions, patent medicines, spices, and small kitchen wares…he was not only too old but also way too short.

The tall man with the pale face, accompanied by his wife, two kids, and an old maid aunt, was probably a bookkeeper bringing his family to the "big city" for a day of penny-wise shopping and seeing the sights. The burly fellow with the callused hands and black pores in his nose had to be a coal miner come to look for work in the Illinois mines. The bookkeeper was too tall, the miner too big and heavy.

Again, no man who disembarked came close to resembling the crafty killer. When it looked as if the last passenger had come ashore, Ward ambled over to a spot behind a board fence to peek through a crack. He wanted to make sure the shrewd killer hadn't waited long enough for a lookout to give up and go away. Ten minutes later when no late departing passenger had come down the plank, he strolled across the street to get a cup of coffee.

When he stepped inside the eating place he immediately spotted the bookkeeper and his family seated at a table waiting to be served. But the old maid aunt wasn't sitting with them…she had probably gone to the toilet out back.

The waitress smiled at the handsome ex-captain of cavalry just as she'd been doing every day for the last four, served him a cup of black coffee and thanked him sweetly for his tip.

Ward stirred his coffee and took a couple of sips. He then glanced at the bookkeeper and his family again and saw that the old maid aunt had not returned. His mind went back to when he'd first seen the family group coming down the gangplank…nobody had seemed to be paying much attention to the old aunt. What was it he had noticed about her that hadn't seemed right?

Suddenly it came to him! Her hair was black, her eyebrows were black but her eyelashes were blond! Almost white! The slippery devil had blacked his brows and disguised himself as a woman but he hadn't put enough shoe polish on his eye lashes!

He disturbed everybody in the room when he jumped to his feet and rushed to the door. He ran to his horse, leaped in the saddle and urged ol' Buck to give his utmost.

He'd never be able to forgive himself for letting the clever devil slip past him.…Some killer catcher he'd turned out to be!

*   *   *

Gideon P. Haliburton, past master in the art of assassination, deception and sabotage, smiled with grim satisfaction as he went about stripping off the outer layer of female garments. He congratulated himself for his ingenious idea of passing himself off as someone's old maid aunt. He had patiently waited on the Kentucky side most of the morning, looking for just the right family to attach himself to.

When he had removed the last bit of female clothing and had re-disguised himself, he calmly walked out of the alley with a man's black wig, beard and moustache all in place. He then strolled over to the livery stable where he rented a saddle horse…a black gelding with a look of breeding about him…a fine looking steed that a gentleman could ride without feeling like a grubby farmer riding a plow horse.

He unhurriedly left town with the blooded horse he'd chosen going at an easy-riding, gentleman's pace. A pace that no one would ever connect with an assassin bent on putting a quick end to a black servant girl that had heard too much…and maybe a meddlesome Quaker girl, too.

He remembered reading in a Confederate Intelligence report about a brash Quaker girl who had incensed a lot of Southern planters by stealing their slaves and spiriting them north beyond the reach of Southern lawmen. It had been reported that she had lived, or had at least laid low between jobs, at the same place where Emily said he'd find Jo.

Any female, even a prim "Thee" and "Thou" Quaker girl who helped slaves escape, deserved no more mercy than a man who committed the same crime. If she happened to be at the Clancy Inn and things looked favorable, he'd even the score for some of his Southern friends, and at the same time give the holier-than-thou Yankees another martyr to mourn.

Goody-goody Quakers with their fanaticism about freedom for half-civilized niggers—no more than two or three generations removed from apes—had always irritated him….Almost as much as the ugly ogre who'd wormed his way into the Presidency so he could destroy the South!

"What a triumph of justice John Booth has wrung from the dregs of defeat and given to all true Southerners!" Gideon had chortled when he heard of the crazed Booth's murderous deed. But if he was lucky enough to find the Quaker female who thought she had sprouted balls, he'd wring some more satisfaction from the dregs of defeat, and give her a dose of Southern justice as well!

He rounded a turn in the road, saw Clancy's Inn up ahead, and slowed his horse to a walk. He took a small mirror from his pocket to see that his wig, beard and moustache were all still in place. He then made sure that his two guns and the slim-bladed dagger concealed under his loose-fitting coat were positioned exactly right. Because it dealt death silently, the dagger was his favorite weapon, but he never hesitated to use one of his expertly crafted pistols if the situation called for it.

He was pleased to see no horses, buggies, or wagons standing by out front. Since it was well past noon, there was a good chance there'd be no late diners to interfere with his vital mission.

He wrapped the bridle reins around the hitching rail, dusted himself off just as any squire would do, stepped to the door with unhurried self-assurance and quietly pushed it open. Once inside he paused to let his eyes become accustomed to the dimmer light.

There was no one sitting at any table. In fact he saw no one at all but he heard the clatter of dishes in the kitchen. He seated himself at a table against the back wall where he'd have a clear view of the front entrance and the door to the cookery.

"Are there any more salt shakers to be filled?"

Ah. It was a young white woman's voice! Could it be the Quaker girl's?

"No, Ma'am. Dis is all of 'um."

Could that be Jo?

What a stroke of luck it would be to find them both here...so alone, and so vulnerable. He'd soon know...the maid should be out in a moment with the refilled shakers.

As the villainous killer sat waiting for the maid to appear with the shakers, Ward rounded the last turn in the road, saw the strange horse at the hitching rail, and slowed Buck to an easy canter. If the killer was there he wanted to get the drop on him and prevent a big shoot-out with bullets flying all around....

When Jo finally pushed through the kitchen door with the shakers, she saw the late-arriving patron seated against the back wall. She instantly recognized the killer by his cold, white-lashed eyes!...It took Gideon an instant longer to recognize Jo....

Ward paused for a moment just outside the door to close his eyes and let them get used to less light. While they were still closed, he heard Jo yell, "It's him!" just as she hurled a salt shaker at the killer's head.

Having to dodge the shaker that was coming straight at his head threw Gideon's aim off and his shot was not fatal. But the witness-killer quickly re-cocked his pistol…the shaker had made him miss his target by a few inches, but he'd put his next bullet exactly where he wanted it.…The disloyal wench would never testify against his sister or anybody else!

But as the killer was taking his deadly aim, Ward shoved the door open and leaped inside. The slug from his big .45 crashed into the killer's chest before he could get off the shot that would have put a bullet in Jo's heart.

The unconscionable killer slumped in his chair with an expression of wide-eyed disbelief on his face. He couldn't believe what was happening…he couldn't be coming to such an inglorious, disesteeming end…not at the hands of a nigger maid and a Yankee blue belly!

He struggled to bring his gun back on target, but he was instantly hammered by another slug from another quarter. The sound of the blast that propelled that hot slug was the last sound he would ever hear. And the last thing he would ever see was a Quaker girl's grim face behind the muzzle flash of Ward's old horse pistol.

Ward and Sina write finis to one of Satan's deadliest killers by grimly blowing the smoke from the barrels of their guns. A member from each of the three groups that Gideon rated lowest on his scumbag list had done him in!…a Quaker girl, a nigger maid, and a Yankee blue belly! Ward figured that ol' Giddy was on his way to Hell with a mighty bitter taste in his mouth.

Sina had followed Jo to the door to take a peek at their mid-afternoon customer. And since most women just naturally look at a man's eyes first, she saw the white lashes and knew that he was the killer an instant before Jo screamed.

She had reached for Ward's old horse pistol hanging by the door, but by the time she had it out of its holster and cocked, Ward had already leaped into the room and fired. But with no hesitation Sina had pulled the trigger when she saw the determined killer trying to shoot Jo again.

As the soulless killer was collapsing on the floor, Sina rushed to Jo, caught her in her arms, and eased her into a chair.

"Jo, are you hurt bad," she asked.

"I don't know," Jo replied, with a weak smile, "it's here in my side..."

Sina gently lifted her bloody blouse, and said, "Thank God. His bullet just grazed a rib...lie still while I get a bandage."

When she came back through the kitchen door with a bandage, she looked at Ward for the first time. He shrugged and she heard him say, "I'm sorry I was a little late..."

Sina smiled a queasy little smile, and said, "Yes, but I'm glad you got here when you did...you know that old pistol of yours misfires sometimes."

Ward nodded his head and while Sina was applying the bandage to Jo's side, he walked over and asked how she was.

"She is going to be all right," Sina assured him, "his bullet just grazed a rib....She recognized him the instant she saw him, and threw a salt shaker that spoiled his aim."

When Jo was all bandaged up and resting easy in a chair, Ward took Sina in his arms, and said, "Sina, Honey, I'm so glad everything has come out all right...I would've been blaming myself for the rest of my life if he had killed you and Jo. He had disguised himself as a woman, and was already on his way out of town when I finally realized the old lady I'd seen comin' off th' boat had white eye lashes."

"It's all right, Darling," Sina kissed him as she whispered the words, "men don't take much notice of a woman's eyes like women do of men's...I got careless myself when I let Jo get out of the kitchen. So don't feel bad about it...let's just be glad we saved Jo and that Mother had already left for town...

"We can also be glad that Miss Emily will soon be getting her just deserts.... When they exhume Mister Andy's body and find all of that morphine she forced him to take, she will wind up in prison, and the Garrisons will get all of his property back…meanwhile, we will be long gone for Texas."

Ward smiled, hugged her tight, and said, "Then you have finally decided for sure that you are ready to accept my proposal?"

When Sina smiled, and said "Yes", he hugged her even tighter and solemnly proclaimed, "What a treasure thou art."

Chapter 10

The old J.P. who had shrewdly located his court across the road from the Inn, united them in holy wedlock the next day. Two days later they said tearful good byes to Sina's mother and their friend, Jo.

They had promised Mrs. McGee that they would be coming back for a visit in a year or two with a grandson for her to dandle on her knee. And then, in just a few years, when railroads had been laid into Texas, they'd be visiting back and forth two or three times a year.

They'd had a serious talk about the money Sina had stashed away. Money that she and some friends (who had later given their all for the cause of freedom) had taken from Garrison agents and heartless bounty hunters....Most of it from Garrison agents who were delivering money to horse thieves who'd stolen horses for Emily to resell to the army, but also some goodly amounts from bounty hunters on their way back home with their pockets stuffed full of slavemaster money.

"Why don't you leave it here for your mother to use in helping ex-slaves find homes and jobs," Ward had suggested.

Sina had gazed out the window and thought about it for a long while before she finally said, "No, I think we have done our share for the slaves...fighting and killing and risking our lives. Now that the war to free them has been fought and won, they are more or less wards of the government, so let them step in and start helping.

"It's high time we started thinking about our own lives, and our own future," she revealed the practical side of her nature.

"Anyway," she went on, "every dollar of that money was either going to Missouri renegades who were selling stolen horses, or had come from plantation owners who had paid bounty hunters for the return of escaped slaves. The biggest part of it, of course, had come right out of Miss Emily's bank account as intended payment for horses the Garrisons sold to both armies at fraudulent prices. I think it is nothing but right for you to take it as an advance share of your inheritance. If you hadn't come along you know who would have wound up with everything, don't you?"

"Yeah," Ward said, "Miss Emily and that son-of-Satan brother of hers."

"You could even say it's a commission for saving the family fortune from two murderous thieves..."

"All right," Ward had given in with a teasing laugh, "you've come up with more than enough reasons for us to take it....All of that, plus my winnings at the poker table, plus our share of the reward we should be gettin' for givin' Gideon P. Haliburton his comeuppance, should be enough to give us a good start in the ranchin' business.

"You know," he added, "it's kinda funny the way things have turned out. I was aimin' t' ask my grandmother for a loan, but now, with all of that other money, we won't be needin' it...but you can go on remindin' me of how deservin' I am."

His feisty Quaker wife had pinched him on his stomach while she was giving him a loving kiss.

Chapter 11

It was about the middle of May when they crossed the Mississippi River into the boot heel of Southeast Missouri.

After leading their horses off the ferry and on up to the top of the high west bank, they paused to look out over the wide expanse of strange land they were about to ride into. Finally, when they had taken in all they could see of the strange, unfamiliar land and had done some wondering as to what might be lying ahead, they "came back" to the present to hold hands and smile reassuringly at each other.

"We may be standing on the exact same spot Mom and Dad stood on twenty-four years ago when they were looking at what we're lookin' at right now." Ward's eyes got misty as he mused…

"And right down there," he went on, "may be the very same dock where they bought a boat for a young slave who had just escaped from a plantation here in Missouri. They knew that after rowing up along th' bank far enough to keep th' current from carryin' him down to Tennessee by the time he got to the other shore, he had a good chance of paddling across to freedom."

Sina gazed up the wide muddy river, and in her ever-romantic soul she could see the desperate youth alone against the world in his little pirogue, paddling across the swollen river to the land of freedom!

"What a beautiful story," she whispered, as her mind and heart finally returned to the less poetic, mundane world around them.

"Yeah," Ward said, as he squeezed her hand, "I knew you'd like it...I've been waitin' 'til we got here to tell it to you."

When they were back in their saddles and were about to start their horses down the long trail to Texas, Sina took a long, last look back toward home....

The first leg of the long track led them down through the boot heel of Missouri into the jungle-like lands of Northeast Arkansas. Where the trail was wide enough, they'd ride side by side and hold hands. When night came, they'd snuggle in their bedrolls spread on patches of grass beside the trail, or in some lumpy bed in a barn-like wayside inn.

By the second day their routine had become pretty well fixed. They would alternately ride an hour and walk half an hour until noon, or until they came to the next stream or a spring beside the road. They'd stop there for an hour to water and feed their horses, while they lunched on some beans and jerky topped off by a few bites of dried fruit for desert. It was the same routine for the rest of the day except for a little better supper prepared over a campfire, or bought in some scrungy inn.

Their favorite line of talk, whether they were riding or walking, was about the house and life they were going to build together in Texas. Besides all of the good feelings they got from their planning, it was a good way to keep their minds off the violence and killing that had plagued the last four years of their lives. They hoped and prayed that such violence and killing was all behind them.

After four days on the jungle-like trail, Sina—remembering all of the violence that had dogged their lives—once again gave heartfelt thanks for their lives, and then reminded Ward that they hadn't needed to fire a shot at anything except a stubborn bull alligator. The old "King of the Swamp" had laid claim to a sunny spot on the trail, and his tail had to be peppered with a load of bird shot before he'd yield enough of it for them to get by.

One morning as they rode along under a sky that was made even bluer by the white fluffy clouds that were drifting along with the breeze, they came up on a totally unexpected scene—a crew of blacks hoeing cotton in a field beside the road...

"Would you look at that?" Sina exclaimed, "I'll bet they have not been told that they have been freed, and are still being held in slavery!"

Seething with indignation, she slid from her saddle and went marching straight to the nearest worker. Ward hooked a leg over his saddle horn and settled back to watch his little Quaker wife do some righting of a wrong.

"Is this the same plantation you were bound to when the war began?" he heard her ask a big black woman who was wielding a hoe with the easy skill of one who'd had long experience with the crop-tending tool.

"Yassum," the woman replied without pausing in her work.

"Have you not been told that the war is over, and you are now free?" Sina asked.

"Yassum, we heerd 'bout that." The woman glanced up to acknowledge Sina's "extraordinary tidings" and then went right back to her work.

"And you are still here? Slaving in the same fields?" Sina was becoming impatient with the too-passive woman's unruffled answers. "Then you must surely be getting pay for the work you are doing?"

The woman paused again to look up and say, "Mistah Babson say he'll settle up with us this fall, when th' cotton is all picked and sold."

"Oh, I'll just bet he will." Sina scoffed sarcastically. "Meanwhile," she pursued the matter like a determined terrier on the trail of a freebooting rat, "how are you getting by, now?"

"We still lives in our cabins for free, and he feeds us well," the still unperturbed woman replied.

"Ha! I just know he does?" Sina tossed her head in disbelief.

Exceedingly skeptical, she turned to a girl in the next row, and said, "Tell me...what did you have for breakfast this morning?"

"Cawnpone and 'lasses," the buxom wench replied without hesitation.

"Ha!" Sina scoffed, "some breakfast to slave on all morning."

Before she could go on with her righteous attempt to set things right, a man came riding up on a big black horse and said, real friendly like, "Good mornin'…what can I do for you folks?"

"There is nothing you can do for us, Sir," Sina replied with fire in her eye and scorn in her voice, "it's what you should do for these people you are still holding in bondage."

"Well, Ma'am," the feller drawled, not at all upset by her obvious intent to charge him with thumbing his nose at the Emancipation Proclamation, "they are no longer slaves, they…"

At that point Sina snatched the whip that was coiled around his saddle horn, and shouted, "Maybe not in name, but I see you still keep the same old scourge close to hand!"

And to clearly demonstrate her implacable opposition to the use of such a scourge on any humankind, she threw the whip on the ground and started stomping on it like a mustang trampling a snake.

Mr. Babson got down from his horse and tried to dissuade Sina from trampling his beautifully crafted whip in the black dirt. But while he was trying to save his whip, her feet got tangled in its coils and she fell over backwards.

When Ward saw the man getting off his horse, he started getting off ol' Buck. And when he saw Sina fall down, he thought the man had pushed her. So, just as any red-blooded husband would do, he walked over and hit Mr. Babson with his fist.

And while "Simon Legree" was lying on the ground out cold from the blow Ward had dealt him, Sina grabbed Ward's knife from his belt and proceeded to cut the long, artfully plaited whip into useless little pieces.

But when she saw "slavemaster" Babson coming back to life, she stopped about two feet from the handle and, with a righteous gleam in her eye, lashed him across his buttocks with the shortened whip.

"How did that feel on your backside, Mr. Slave Driver?…Just because slaves are black, doesn't mean they feel any less pain and humiliation than you do," she sternly upbraided the villainous abuser of humankind.

As the chastised exploiter of poor simple-minded slaves rubbed his behind, Sina hurled the remains of his whip into the scummy waters of a ditch.

While Sina was cutting up "Simon's" whip, she'd hardly noticed the two black women who had quietly moved in to lift Mr. Babson's head and start wiping the dirt off his face. When she had thrown his whip and looked back around, she saw that one of the women was the one who had so steadfastly refused to be stampeded into rebellion.

The woman looked up at Sina and said in her still calm, unruffled way, "The whip was not for us...he popped it t' scare th' crows out of th' corn patch. As for what Cassie had for breakfas', she jes' likes cawnpone and 'lasses....I had beans and grits and sowbelly just like Mistah Babson and ever'body else had. He's a good man, and he'll take care of us. So please don't give him no mo' trouble."

Sina looked around at the other blacks and saw that most of them were nodding in agreement with what their spokeswoman had said.

Ward heard the sob that Sina tried to muffle as she grabbed up her hat and ran to her horse.

*   *   *

They rode along beside each other with no word being spoken for nearly a mile. Finally, Ward reached over and took Sina's hand and that's when the dam broke and the tears came streaming down...

"Oh, Ward," she wailed, "I am so ashamed I could die!"

He quickly dismounted, took her down in his arms and held her close.

"It's all right," he comforted her. "There at the end I think everybody saw how bad you felt about the mistake you'd made. If it'll make you feel any better, I gave Mr. Babson ten dollars to buy himself a new whip."

"Ward," she sobbed, "I promise that from this day on, I'm going to do my best to control my Irish temper."

"Honey," Ward drawled, "I sure hope you do, else you're gonna be givin' th' Quakers a bad name, and what's more, you're gonna be gettin' me in an awful lot of fights!"

They kissed and held each other tight…sharing their love heart-to-heart in the middle of a road beside a murky bayou in Eastern Arkansas.

Chapter 12

After a long restful night on a thick featherbed in a nice hotel in Little Rock, they dallied too long over breakfast and were late getting back on the road. The sun had set and it was already getting dark when they rode into Benton, the county seat of Saline County. They signed the register for the last room in the town's only inn.

When he came out to meet them, they gave the old hostler precise instructions for the care and feeding of their horses. He immediately saw that their mounts were from quality stock and he appreciated their concern for their proper care. They saw that he could be trusted and gave him a generous tip.

After they had bathed and dressed, they came down to a fine meal the Benton Inn hostess had so graciously put together for them. With her cook having already gone home, Mrs. Brazil had prepared most of it herself from scratch. She acknowledged with a smile her hungry guests' complimentary comments.

The proprietress of the Benton Inn was in her mid-thirties....A little on the buxom side but not yet old enough to be described as "motherly". The strand of hair that had strayed from under her maid-style cap was light brown, her eyes were blue and when she smiled they sparkled with friendliness. All of which, coupled with her amiable disposition, suited her well for the inn-keeping business.

"I'll bet you two have just got married, and I'll bet you are now on your way to Texas." Mrs. Brazil made the friendly observation as she refilled their glasses with more fresh milk.

"I am pleased to say you are exactly right, Ma'am," Ward proudly acknowledged the correctness of her observation, "I was born and brought up in Brushy Creek, 'bout twenty miles southwest of San Antonio....Don't hold it against her," he nodded toward Sina, "but she's a Yankee from Illinois."

"Oh, I won't," Mrs. Brazil laughed, "since she was smart enough to marry a Texan and come south to live."

Sina smiled sweetly but under the table she stomped on Ward's foot.

Being discreet in such matters, Sina didn't reveal the fact that Ward had been a Union officer, and had outfitted himself with some more or less Texas-style clothes before they left Cairo. He had agreed that there was not much use in inviting trouble in Rebel states by wearing a blue uniform. But Sina suspected that he would have worn one if she hadn't been along.

"But I'm afraid," their hostess went on as she glanced around as if she was making sure the walls hadn't sprouted ears, "we may now have too many of the wrong kind comin' south to live—or you could say to live off of us.—To pick our bones some folks are saying."

Ward's face took on a grave look as he said, "What do you mean by that, Ma'am?"

"Well," Mrs. Brazil said, after another glance around to make sure the room was still vacant except for them, "I mean the way the Yankee army billets its soldiers on us and confiscates any property they want."

Ward laid his fork down, looked his hostess straight in the eye, and said, "You have personal knowledge of this?"

Mrs. Brazil lifted her chin, and said, "Huh. I reckon I do. There are two Yankee officers billeted on me right now, and there are at least two dozen soldiers quartered in homes around town. And that's sayin' nothin' about a whole squad of blue bellies they have billeted at my father-in-law's place a mile out of town."

"A squad of soldiers in your father-in-law's house?" Ward couldn't believe what she was saying. "Why so many on him?"

"Well," she replied, "I'm sure it's because he was a member of the state legislature who staunchly supported the South with his speeches and strong words. And maybe, too, because he was the biggest slave-holder in th' county.

"Anyway, it wasn't enough for them that he had lost two sons—one was my husband—and most of his property. They have to further humiliate him my making him house and feed ten or twelve foul-mouthed blue bellies, who drink and carouse around most of every night."

Ward didn't want to believe what the woman was saying, but he couldn't shake the feeling that she was telling the truth....Vindictiveness was another one of those vestigial traits that men still carried in their primitive baggage. He remembered, though he knew it didn't make it right, that the Confederates had confiscated property, and had lorded it over conquered civilians in a few places, themselves.

Even so, he wished the woman hadn't made him so keenly aware of the wrongs that some part of the army was committing. He was no part of it now and he had never bullied a conquered foe. He and Sina had settled a few scores for the slaves and had put the Marlin Garrisons back on the right track....All he wanted now was for the two of them to be able to forget and live in peace—to say nothing of them wanting to enjoy their wayfaring honeymoon, and get on home to Brushy Creek.

Ward shoved his chair back rather abruptly, got to his feet, and said, "Goodnight, Ma'am. We have t' get some sleep. We have another long ride ahead of us tomorrow."

On their way to their room Sina took Ward's arm, and said, "Ward, Honey, I know that all came as a shock to you. It was a shock to me, too, but what can I say? In every army there are those men who are not sat-isfied with just conquering, they must also humiliate, even persecute."

"I guess so," Ward said, "but I look on such actions as an offense to the good men who fought and died at Shiloh, Sharpstown, and Gettesburg. I know that no survivor of any of those battles could ever humiliate a conquered foe. I'll bet," he went on bitterly, "there's not an officer or a man in this occupying detachment who has ever been in a real battle."

"Probably not," Sina readily agreed.

*　　　　　*　　　　　*

Their war-widowed hostess had just served their breakfast the next morning, when two Union officers came parading into the dining room. The one leading the parade was a young major, resplendent in a gold-braided uniform that would have made a Mexican General's best get-up look shoddy. Ward could see "West Point" stamped all over him.

He was about 26 or 27, clean-shaved except for a trimmed-to-perfec-tion military mustache, grown, no doubt, to make him appear more mature and speed his rise through the ranks. A cavalry officer's pistol on one hip, and a saber on the other arrogantly augmented his too-grandiose attire.

The pompous major's second-lieutenant aide was not yet out of his teens and was still plagued with adolescent pimples. It looked as if he had shaved a few times but had left all of the fuzz on his upper lip, which he was no doubt trying to nurture to more mature proportions to emulate his superior. He was most likely fresh out of some prep school, and his commission had no doubt been wangled by a daddy with a lot of influence.

The two peacocky "conquerors", who in all likelihood had never set foot on a battlefield, took seats at a table in a far corner of the room, removed their spotless hats and gloves and looked around impatiently for someone to take their orders.

An unsmiling Mrs. Brazil slow-footed it over to their table with her pad and pencil. She was obviously not overjoyed with their non-paying business. Not only had they never paid for a meal, they had never even left her a tip.

"Those two men at that table over there," the major arrogantly inquired, "have you already taken their orders?"

"Yes, I have," Mrs. Brazil replied.

"What are they having, and are their orders about ready?" the bumptious major went on to ask.

"Ham and eggs and biscuits, and yes they are about ready." Mrs. Brazil hated having to tell.

"All right," the would-be Napoleon brusquely ordered, "since our time is much more valuable than theirs, bring us their breakfast without delay, and fix two more for them."

"Yes, Sir," Mrs. Brazil mumbled as she turned and began slow-footing it to the kitchen. She glanced apologetically at her two long-time patrons who would now have to wait through another preparation time. They responded with understanding nods.

Sina put her hand on Ward's arm and gave him a "this-is-no-time-or-place-for-heroics" look. The tension in his arm relaxed, and she breathed a little prayer of thanks. If he tried to interfere she was sure he'd be stood up against a wall and shot as soon as a firing squad could be assembled, and the arrogant Major shout "Fire!".

Still moving at her snail's pace, Mrs. Brazil finally came out of the kitchen with the two breakfasts the Yankee major had so autocratically usurped. As she was setting them on the table before the two detestable "conquerors", the cocky major looked up with a smirky smile, and said, "Thank you. Your prompt service is appreciated." The fawning aide stroked his superior's ego with a muffled snicker.

Ward and Sina had to force down every bite of the sumptuous breakfast Mrs. Brazil had prepared for them....They knew they couldn't ride all morning on empty stomachs.

When they had finally choked the last bites down through anger-constricted throats, they went back to their room to pack their belongings. They knew they had to put some distance between them and Yankee-occupied Benton before their violated senses of fairness and decency exploded and put them in big trouble.

When they returned to pay their bill, they were glad to see that the peacocky major and his subservient little flunky had already left the premises. They thanked Mrs. Brazil for her hospitality, said goodbye, and headed for the corral to get their horses. They were glad that they had told the hostler to get them ready.

As they approached the stables that adjoined the corral, they met the two arrogant officers they were hoping to avoid. Just seeing them again was enough to irritate Ward, but his hackles really bristled when he saw the cock-robin major sitting high in the saddle on Buck!

Just like any Texan who saw a thief making off with his horse, Ward reached for his gun. But he remembered the touchy circumstances they were in, thought better of it, and while forcing himself to speak in a controlled voice, he said, "Pardon me, Major, but you seem to have mounted the wrong horse."

Major Dundren glanced at his aide and with condescending humor, he said, "Can you believe it, Winfred? Here is a local rustic who hasn't heard that Union majors don't make mistakes. Recite for him the hard facts of living under the authority of an occupying army, and the privileges certain officers can exercise at their discretion."

"Major Dundren has confiscated your horse, which the Area Commander has the authority to do," Winfred promptly translated with a big smirk.

Ward put his hand on Buck's reins, and started to explain that he was an ex-union officer himself. But before he could get the first word out,

Major Dundren indignantly commanded, "Take your hand off my horse's reins!" And to reinforce his order, he reached for his saber with the clear intention of hacking Ward's hand off at the wrist!

But his shiny, parade ground saber never cleared its scabbard because Ward hauled him from his saddle and slammed him on the ground! When the befuddled major started feeling around for his parade ground saber, Ward stomped on it with the heel of his boot and snapped the blade off at the handle.

The arrogant major had not yet learned that giving up a fight was sometimes better than foolhardy valor....With a reckless lack of discretion, he started pawing for his pistol as he struggled to his feet. Ward set himself, waited for just the right moment, and busted his jaw with his big right fist!

Lieutenant Winfred Holifield, II, finally recovered from the shock of seeing his superior being so rudely manhandled, and made an unwise move for his gun. Bravely supporting his fallen commander could net him a quick promotion.

"Let it alone, Junior!" Sina warned with the sure promise of instant death in the tone of her voice. And when the glory-seeking, still-wet-behind-the-ears lieutenant found himself looking into the muzzle of a rock-steady .38 revolver, he wet his pants and fell off his horse in a dead faint!

"Come on," Ward said, "let's get 'em out of sight."

They hurriedly dragged the two out-cold oppressors to the back of a stall, gagged them with pieces of burlap cut from feed bags, and then tied them to two stout posts. They couldn't help smiling at the thought of them waking up with the stench of manure in their noses, and their fancy uniforms smeared with wet stable muck!...Their fancy garbs would have to be burned!

When the young aide showed signs of coming around, Ward said— for him to hear and pass on— "I was a captain of cavalry in General

Grant's army....I do hope I won't have to seek his help in putting the squelch on any court martial somebody may want to convene."

Young Winfred's eyes went wide with the mere thought of it, and he rolled his head from side to side in an emphatic denial that anything like that would never happen.

They rushed to their horses and mounted up, but not wanting to attract any undue attention, they left town at a moderate canter. But when they were past the last house on the road out of town, they urged their horses into a much faster pace. They wanted to put as much distance as they could between them and the troops that were sure to be coming after them—just as soon as Major Dundren could get that burlap gag out of his mouth!

What an ironic twist of fate! Little more than a month back, Ward had been fighting die-hard Confederates, today he had assaulted a Union Major! He knew he had been in the right both times, but even so, should he be caught he knew he'd be hauled before a Union firing squad...and Sina's fate could be even worse!

They rode hard all morning and it was after noon before they finally stopped looking over their shoulders every other minute. They stopped their tired horses beside a little stream and dismounted to loosen saddle girths so their horses could relax, drink some water, and get a few minutes rest.

While they were dismounted Ward put his little spyglass back in his saddlebag. He had used it to check their back trail from several high points along the way, and he had been a little more relieved each time when he saw no mounted blue coats in hot pursuit. Having good horseflesh under them had given them a comfortable lead...He figured they could maintain their lead—maybe even increase it— if one of their horses didn't go lame...

They munched on some jerky, refilled their canteens and rode on at a little slower pace. But an hour or so later when they had topped another high place, Ward got his little glass out again. After carefully focusing and scanning and seeing no sign of hard-riding blue coats spurring their horses in hot pursuit, he was relieved even more.

But he couldn't believe that neither of the trussed-up dandies had worked himself free, or the old hostler hadn't found them....He grinned when it finally dawned on him that the old hostler might have seen the two blue bellies getting kinks put in their tails, and had purposely found a backlog of chores that needed to be done in other places. The arrogant dandies might not be found before the evening muster.

But even though Ward had confidently concluded that no posse was in hot pursuit, they prudently denied themselves the comfort of wayside inns for the next two nights, and slept off the trail deep in heavy woods.

Chapter 13

With stiff necks from having taken so many anxious looks over their shoulders when they were riding for their lives out of Benton, they crossed the Red River into Texas on the twenty-fourth day of May.

When they were off the ferry and back in their saddles, Sina looked at Ward, and teased, "Where are all of those great Texas plains you've been telling me about? I can't see anything but big green trees and there's not a cow in sight."

Ward grinned, and said, "Sina, Honey, we are not in th' real Texas yet. The real Texas is hidden behind two hundred miles of trees to make it hard for Yankees to find....It's kinda like it was with Moses and the Children of Israel, you have to push through a lot of wilderness to get to the Promised Land."

"Then lead on 'Moses,'" Sina smiled at him, "wherever you want to 'pitch your tent' will be the Promised Land for me."

"What a treasure thou art." Ward told her for about the fortieth time as he leaned from his saddle to kiss her—just like he had also done some forty times or more.

Now that they were in Texas, Ward was worrying even less about them being on the run from Major Dundren's vindictive wrath....The threat of him and a troop of cavalry appearing on the horizon behind them was no longer a big source of worry. In fact, he had finally decided that the Peacocky Major had been too proud to let it be known that he had been bested in a fight with a "rustic", and left to be found all trussed up in a stinking horse stall.

He told Sina to stop worrying about any avenging posse being on their tails, and start enjoying her new life in "the Promised Land". No Union troops had ever really invaded Texas, and besides that, everybody back east still looked on Texas as being a land of Indians, Mexicans, renegades, defectors, and rebellious dissidents…none of whom had charitable feelings for outsiders.

"OK, Moses," Sina said, "I'll start doing that.…But since I can't remember the name of the next town, and I have never seen it in the Bible, say it for me again."

"Nac-og-do-ches," Ward pronounced it for her syllable by syllable, "it has a 'g' in it, but it's silent."

*   *   *

They rode into the old Stone-Fort town with its unpronounceable Indian name just after noon the next day. They signed the register in the same old hostelry that John and Laura had lodged in on their trek to Texas back in '41.

The young proprietor—who had already learned the value of good public relations—proudly produced the register for that year and they soon found the page where John and Laura Garrison had signed their names on May 28, 1841.

The next morning, as Ward was hanging around the blacksmith shop waiting for their horses to be shod, he spotted three ex-confederates in rebel gray riding down the street. They were probably on their way home just as he was and should present no problem. But when he finally saw who they were, he immediately canceled the thought about them being no problem.

The three riders were not just any three hangdog ex-confederates on their way home from the war. They were Tom and Wes Clark and their nursemaid/bodyguard, Luther Tucker. And the hometown they were headed for was the same as his, Brushy Creek.

From their well-fed looks Ward was sure they had surrendered to the first Union soldier they had seen, and had sat out the war lounging around some Yankee prison camp just as Wes and Tom's daddy, Bascom Clark, had instructed.... The old cattle baron hadn't cared a hoot about his boys fighting for "a bunch of cotton-farming secessionists and their niggers", but he knew they had to sign up for appearance sake.

He had sent Luther Tucker, his top gun hand, along as insurance in helping his sons survive the every-man-for-himself conditions that he knew existed in some prison camps. They might take Luther's gun away, but Bascom knew that "nursemaid" Luther knew a dozen ways to quietly kill anyone who appeared to be a threat to one of his boys.

When they had been released at war's end, Ward guessed that they had come down the Natchez Trace and then on to Natchitoches, Louisiana to follow the Old Spanish Trail to Nacogdoches, where—as unkind fate would have it—their trail had merged in time and space with his and Sina's.

If they should spot him, they would very likely grab the chance to get revenge for his daddy testifying against Wes in his trial for attempted murder. The Jury had found him guilty, but Bascom had bribed the judge and got him a probated sentence.

If he and Sina could have been just a day or two ahead of them—or vice versa.

He stepped back into the blacksmith shop to avoid being seen. But he hadn't moved soon enough. Weasel-eyed Wes' had already spotted him.

Ward read his lips when he said to Tom and Luther, "There's Ward Garrison...he was on th' Yankee side. Let's let him know that he ain't whipped us, yet!"

But Luther said, "Not now...too many people around. He's on his way home...down th' trail we'll pick our spot and nobody will ever know..."

Ward let them ride on by without saying anything. Had he been traveling alone he would've had it out with them right then and there. But knowing that one of them might get off a lucky shot, leaving Sina all alone in a strange town full of homebound ex-soldiers all aching for a woman, he decided against it.

When the smithy had re-shod the last one of their horses, Ward rode back to the inn and put their horses back in the corral.

Sina had replenished their trail supplies at the local store, and was back in their room packing for another long day on the trail.

"Hold off on your packin'," Ward told her as he walked into the room with a glum look on his face, "we'll be stayin' another night."

"Staying another night?" Sina was naturally surprised, "I know we had a lot of fine fun last night in that springy bed, but I thought you were anxious to get home."

"I am," Ward said, "but something has come up..."

He went on to tell her about seeing and being seen by the Clark brothers and their hired gunman and the danger they presented.

When he had finished, Sina asked, "Is there another trail we can take?"

"Not one that won't take us a hundred miles out of our way," he replied. "And even on that trail," he went on, "we could be waylaid by outlaws or a band of Indians who'd be just as ready to jump us."

He turned his back, looked out the window, and said, "Maybe we ought t' stay here two or three days or a whole week, and let them get tired of lying in ambush waitin' for us."

Sina stood silent for a long moment while Ward stood with his back to her. Finally, she said, "If I wasn't with you, you wouldn't wait, would you? In fact, you would have already had it out with them out there in the street, wouldn't you?

"Ward Garrison, you were no fraidy cat when I married you, and I don't want you turning into one now—certainly not on my account. We may already have half the Union army on our tails so what would you rather we do? Face a Union firing squad or take our chances with two cowards and one nursemaid? You ought to know by now that I don't run from fights, and I sure don't want to be married to a man that does!"

Ward wheeled around, swept her up in his arms, and said, "You gutsy little Irish hellion! I guess I had that comin'. I should have known you'd rather fight 'em than try t' dodge 'em. —But we do need to stay another night to plan strategy and get ready for them....Besides, our horses can use another day's rest just as we can."

Sina put her arms around his neck, and said, "Why don't we do some more of that 'resting' right now?"

Ward said, "What a treasure thou art!"

Chapter 14

"Yeah, I seen 'em…passed by here yestiddy", was the answer they most often got to the question they put to everyone they saw along the trail.

So the vengeance-seeking Clark brothers and their hired gun were still a day ahead of them looking for just the right spot. Which meant that they had to keep on approaching every grove of trees along the trail with great caution…sometimes with Ward scouting ahead, his gun drawn and ready. They well knew that the three killers could camp overnight in one of a hundred draws beside the trail, and ambush them the next morning…

They made it to Crockett where they slept in the new Town Inn their first night out of Nacogadoches. They found another wayside inn down the trail the second night, and made it to Bryan the third night where they found lodging in a boardinghouse with a spare room. As they were eating their supper, they were told that three men traveling together had left Bryan late that morning headed for "San Antone".

An all morning but worry-free ride out of Bryan, took them across flat farmland that offered too little cover for ambushers on horseback, and brought them to the ferry landing at the Brazos river.

At the landing there were four crude buildings with sheds attached for stables and temporary storage. And for the easy money he could make dishing out grungy grub for hungry ex-soldiers on their way home from the war, some hustler had set up a big mess tent on the high ground back from the landing.

They saw that the ferry was docking at the far bank. and since they'd have to wait for it to unload and re-cross the river, they decided to see "what was on the menu" under the tent. They tied their horses to the makeshift-hitching rail to which some ten or twelve other horses had already been tied…but with his eye for horses Ward saw that none of them belonged to Wes, Tom, or Luther.

Feeling a little less tensed up, they ducked under the edge of the sagging tent and found a crude table at the back. They seated themselves on a homemade bench, and soon spotted a hefty woman coming their way with a pot of coffee and two big bowls of something they hoped would be edible on a two-foot slab of plank.

She set the loaded "tray" on their table and said, with no word of greeting, "We ain't got no menu cause wild pig stew is all we got. If you want it, it will be five dollars for each bowl—gold or Yankee greenbacks…the coffee is two dollars extra."

Ward looked at Sina, and when she finally gave him a dubious nod, he handed the waitress two fives and two ones of the specified color.

After a cautious peek in his bowl, Ward said, "With all of the wild things they put in this stuff, I bet they had to stir it with a gun barrel to make it stay in th' pot!"

Sina laughed and made an ugly face.

As they were warily tasting the unappealing fare, they noticed a group of black ex-soldiers eating their bowls of "gun barrel" stew just outside the tent in the shade of a big tree. Ward figured they were ex-slaves that had joined the Union Army. He guessed that they were traveling together in a group to discourage attacks by still unreconciled ex-rebs. And since the number of white men he had seen around the landing, just about equaled the number of horses at the hitching rail, they had to be traveling on foot.

Ward suddenly became aware of a commotion at a big table under the far end of the tent where some barbaric looking ruffians were wolfing their stew and guzzling swamp whiskey.

As their talk got louder and their primal passions mounted, Ward began hearing words like, "she", "her", and "woman". Then as the talk got even louder, he heard the dreaded words, "I tell you she is a woman dressed in men's clothes…young and purty, too. Come on let's get her. After two years in prison, I'm ready for a woman!…After me, you all can be next!"

With their guns drawn and lecherous leers on their bearded faces, seven or eight of the barbarous brutes got to their feet and came lurching toward them.

"OK, mister," the lead brute said to Ward, "you just stay out of the way and keep quiet…you can have her back when we get through with her!"

From under the table Ward put a bullet in his black heart. And with indignant righteousness Sina shot another one with the little .38 they had taken from Gideon's lifeless hand. Ward shot the legs out from under another one and that started the others to falling back. With guttural grunts and curses they turned two heavy tables on their sides, and hunkered down behind them.

Ward quickly did the same with their table. But he soon found that not even the bullets from his big .45 could penetrate the slab tops of the tables the ruffians were behind. They did their best, but bobbing heads were hard to hit. In less than a minute their guns were snapping on empty shells.

As they were hurrying to reload, one of the lusting brutes yelled, "Their guns are empty! Come on let's take 'em!"

Ward said, "Let's make a run for our horses!" But he knew they'd never make it…he'd be cut down and the love of his life would be gang raped!

But just as the killer/rapists were getting back on their feet, two of the black ex-soldiers grabbed up pots of hot coffee and dashed the steaming brew on their backs. One of the big ex-soldiers then shouted, "Get to your hosses and get outa heah!"

One of the other blacks handed them their horses' reins and another one picked Sina up and sat her in her saddle.

When they were both in their saddles, the big leader shouted, "Get to the ferry! We'll hold 'em off!"

But Ward shouted back, "No, you run for the ferry with us. If you stay here they'll kill you!" The big fellow hesitated for a moment then hurled the pot he was holding at the brute closest to him.

Ward and Sina spurred their horses for the ferry that was just then docking on the near shore, while the ex-soldiers held off their pursuers by firing and falling back in well ordered movements.

"When all of us get on board, get this ferry headed back to the other shore," Ward ordered the "captain" when he and Sina had ridden on board and dismounted.

"I can't," the "captain" replied, "I'll have to wait 'til I can get up more pressure."

Ward pointed his .45 at him, and said, "Use what you've got...get us as far from this bank as you can!"

When a bullet whizzed past the captain's head, making him fully aware of what was happening, he jumped overboard.

Ward was about to take over the helm when the big leader of the group rushed on deck and said, "Heah, Cap'un, Suh...I learned to run one of these boats in th' army....Henry," he said to one of the other ex-sloldiers in faded blue, "get back there and stoke that fire and shake that grate!...Put anything under that boiler that'll burn and then slosh some of that coal oil on it....Get us some steam so we can get this boat movin'!"

Henry jumped to, and Big John took the helm.

In all of his years in the army, Ward had never seen a man take charge in an emergency so naturally and effectively. Anyone could see that Big John was a born leader.

When the last man was aboard, Big John opened the steam valve all the way. The creaky old boat shuddered and began moving as the old paddle wheels started churning up the water. And as the friendly troops kept the would-be rapists at bay, the rising pressure Henry was coaxing from the old boiler started the old boat to moving a little faster.

With the hot flames from the coal oil pushing the pressure even higher, the churning paddles soon had them beyond the effective range of the frustrated ruffian's guns. When the churning paddles had finally propelled them to safe harbor on the far bank, Big John gave the brutish scofflaws a long defiant blast from the old boat's whistle!

As they were all disembarking, laughing and whooping it up over the way they had frustrated the would-be rapists, Big John went back aboard the old ferry. When he returned a few minutes later, he told Ward, "I disabled the engine....They'll have to make some new parts befo' they can git it runnin' again. I wanted to make sure they wouldn't be able to get hosses across and be comin' after us any time soon."

"Good thinking," Ward said.

With a warm handshake he went on to thank Big John for saving his and Sina's lives. With that done with sincere gratitude, he asked him if they were all going on down the trail to San Antonio.

Big John shook his head, and said, "No, Suh. We is all goin' back home to Richmond, 'bout two hundred miles down river....We'd been waitin' for th' riverboat, but now we'll jus' go downstream a few miles and board it at another landin'."

"By th' way," Ward said, "during your last day or two on th' trail, did you see three white men—one of them ridin' a gray horse—anywhere along th' way?"

"Yassuh, we sho' did," Big John replied, "they passed us 'bout mid-afta' noon yestaday...they musta stayed th' night heah, 'cause we saw 'em boadin' th ferry 'bout ten this mawnin', jes as we wuz getting' heah."

Ward smiled, and said, "Thank you, John. And thanks again for savin' our hides."

Sina stepped up and said, "I want to thank you, too, John." And then with a smile she said to the trooper who had so quickly sat her in her saddle, "Thank you, too...I have never been put in a saddle so quick in my life."

They could still hear Big John and the others laughing and whooping it up as they marched in step around a bend down the trail...celebrating their freedom...proud of what they'd done...

When all of the proud talk and laughter had faded away, Ward and Sina exchanged long looks. They both knew that they had been well paid for all they had done for the slaves...

   *   *   *

That night they camped in a draw on the bank of a little creek. While Sina fixed supper, Ward got out the coil of wire he'd bought in Nacogadoches and strung it up around their camp at just the right height to strip a rider from his saddle.—Especially a coward that was riding in fast to do a dirty deed and then get out fast. With that done, he took the three cowbells he'd bought and hung one from the wire in three places around their camp.

From what Big John had told him he figured the killers were moving slow, waiting for he and Sina to catch up enough for them to be spotted from some high place along the trail. They'd then stay just far enough ahead not to be heard or seen. And just before sundown when they knew their prey would be camping for the night no more than a mile or two behind them, they'd stop, too. Then when it was dark they'd quietly backtrack until they saw a campfire...

But Ward and Sina didn't sleep anywhere near the fire in their camp site. After they had "dined" on their hardtack and beans, they stuffed their bedrolls with leaves and grass to make it look like they were sleeping near the smoldering coals. But with their horses tethered back in the woods well off the trail, they actually went to bed way back from their alarm-rigged camp with their guns laying ready at their sides.

But even with the wire and the bells all in place to protect and give them some warning, it was hard for them to relax and go to sleep. Harrowing visions of their narrow escape from the scofflaws at the ferry kept coming back to their minds. Without the help of Big John and his men they'd have been…well, they both knew what their fate would have been.

But then they'd smile when they remembered the triumphant whoops from Big John and his friends.…After being barred from any actual fighting during the war, they had finally got to strike a blow for what was good and right. What a boost the victory at the ferry must've been for their feelings of self-worth!

The moon rose to give some light. But it was diminished by the new spring leaves that were thick on the boughs overhead, and when some clouds came drifting in from the south the big yellow orb was sometimes blotted out altogether. What a waste Sina sighed resignedly, as she watched the big lover's moon glide along between two fluffy clouds for what must've been two whole minutes…

"What a fine moon for romancing," she mused, "and here we lie side-by-side with all of our clothes on, waiting to kill or be killed."

"Yeah, it's a waste all right," Ward whispered. Then he said, "Since they haven't already hit us, I figure it'll be just before dawn. So let's get some sleep and wake up just before it starts gettin' light." As a soldier-cavalryman he had trained himself to wake up to his own set-to-the-minute internal alarm clock.

Just before midnight a horse nickered. Ward knew immediately that it was ol' Buck…he had no doubt heard something. Were they being crossed up? Were the killers sneaking in on foot, before midnight? He touched Sina to rouse her, and then reached for his gun.

"There could be something or somebody movin' around up there," he whispered. "But it could be some animal that Buck heard…"

A big cloud was blocking out most of the light from the moon so that Ward couldn't see more than a few feet any way he looked. He listened intently for a minute, and then said, "Ol' Buck hasn't nickered again and no bell has jangled, so it must've been nothin'."

"Are you sure it wasn't an Indian?" Sina whispered.

Ward let the hammer down on his gun, and said, "No, I don't think it was an Indian…they don't prowl around much at night."

They re-snuggled themselves in their bedroll, and Ward reset his internal clock to wake him one hour before dawn, which would be the most likely time for a cowardly attack.

But the expected attack didn't come.

The tired, harassed couple didn't know whether to be thankful or disappointed. Since they knew the dreaded attack would come sooner or later they may have felt more disappointed.…They'd just have to face another long day of dread while they stayed constantly on alert.

While Sina cooked breakfast, Ward took his bells down and re-coiled his wire. They were back on the trail soon after sunrise, faced with a long ride across miles of wooded land that presented dozens of good places for bushwhackers to lie in wait.

They went at a slow pace while they watched ahead for disturbed birds. Especially blue jays that might be flitting about fussing at intruders that got too close to their nests. They also kept their eyes on their horses' ears…if their rhythmic, synchronized beat should suddenly stop with the two of them coming to a point, it could mean trouble up ahead.

About mid-afternoon they found themselves in country that was more open…gentle slopes dotted here and there with clumps of mesquite and streaked every mile or so by small tree-lined streams.

Seeing that there wasn't enough cover along most of the streams to hide three bushwhackers on horses, they relaxed their vigilance and started appreciating the fields of blue bonnets, primroses and Indian paintbrushes they'd be riding through the rest of the day.

But by sundown they had ridden back into a more wooded area along a much larger creek. It didn't look like the best of places for them to camp, but they were tired, it was a good place to take a bath, and camping there would be better than riding on in the dark. They found a place with enough trees in the right places for Ward to string up his wires and alarm bells.

It was getting dark under a cloudy sky, and night birds were already warbling their mournful notes by the time the weary pair had warmed up their beans, bacon, and hardtack. When they had eaten their meager fare, Ward poured what was left of their coffee on the fire to dampen it down to just a few smoldering embers. They then put together some grass, leaves, and chunks that would, under a blanket in the dark, look like two tired travelers sleeping by a nearly burned out campfire.

With the wire and bells all positioned just right, they bedded down behind a big tree several yards back from the "sleeping" dummies.

"Sina, Honey," Ward said, when they were all stretched out with his "on-alert" alarm all set, "I'm sorry I have gotten you in all this mess. If something should happen, I…I won't ever be able to forgive myself."

"Hey," Sina said as she came up on one elbow, "I've been in tight places before….We've been in a couple together and we've come through them just fine. Anyway, I knew I wasn't going on a church picnic when I hit the trail to Texas with you….So buck up, Big Boy, we are in the right, and with the wires and bells you've strung up, we have a good chance at getting through this tight spot, too."

Ward kissed her, and then said with a thankful sigh, "What a treasure thou art."

Sina snuggled up against him and just when he thought she was dropping off to sleep, she mumbled, "I love you for worrying about me."

"Sh-h-h," Ward shushed his treasure, "go to sleep...I won't let anything happen to you."

Somewhere around midnight he had to shift himself around to relieve the pressure on his hips and shoulders. While he was fully awake, he lifted his head to listen for a minute....Roosting birds were chirping reassuringly to each other....Buck and their other horses were quietly resting on the bank of the creek, and an owl was contentedly hooting from the top of a tree by the trail....

But when the birds heard the owl hooting, their reassuring chirps instantly changed to chirps of alarm and then there were no chirps at all....A lurking owl meant that one of them might not be around when it came time for them to herald the coming of a new day.

Before laying his head back on his travel-worn pillow he fluffed it up to get some of the lumps out....He knew the critical time would come just before dawn and that would give them a few more hours of "semi-restful" sleep. With an arm across Sina he went back to his "on-alert" dozing.

But something woke him before his internal alarm went off and he immediately saw that dawn was already breaking in the east! He had forgotten how early it started getting light on the plains with summer coming on.

He touched Sina and then cocked his ear toward the trail. The birds had all gone silent again...but because it was time for owls to be "retiring for the day", he was sure it was no owl that had silenced them this time. He finally heard what had woke him...it was the creak of saddle leather.

"Get ready," he whispered to Sina, "this could be it!"

As they were reaching for their guns they heard horses suddenly spurred into fast gallops. And almost at once they saw the dim forms of three riders come charging into their set-up camp. They couldn't help feeling a little intimidated by the bloodcurdling yells from killers who thought they had the advantage of paralyzing surprise.

As they crouched behind the tree and watched in the dim light, they were glad to see the lead rider wiped from his saddle by one of the wires. But the other two riders charged on into the set-up camp, yelling and firing shot after shot into the "bodies" on the ground.

The first rider had no doubt broken a section of Ward's wire, and the other two had ridden in behind him thinking that he'd been knocked from his saddle by a low limb.

The still-mounted riders emptied their guns into the dummies as they rode around the set-up camp. But then as Ward and Sina watched, one of them yelled, "Them's dummies! They have tricked us!...Come on, let's find them, they have t' be around here somewhere."

Ward and Sina took firm grips on their guns and cocked the hammers...their flesh and blood bodies would now become the killer's targets!

But as the two riders wheeled their horses to go looking for their quarry, they ran into another section of wire. And when that wire didn't break they were both wiped from their saddles and dumped on the hard ground just as rudely as the first one had been.

"Well, I'll be damned," Ward said, "it worked just like I thought it might...come on, let's get their guns before they come to."

When they had rushed up to where the three would-be killers were lying stunned on the ground, Ward cocked his gun, pointed it down at the first one's head, and said, "I think I'll just go ahead and finish them off!"

"No!" Sina cried out as she grabbed his arm, "you can't do that! It would be killing in cold blood, and it would make you just as low and inhuman as they are!"

"I say it would be nothin' but justice." Ward growled, as he again tried to bring his gun to bear on Wes' sorry head.

"But it's not right for justice to be dealt out by the intended victims," Sina pleaded as she hung to his arm, "let's let the law and the courts deal with them."

"I don't want t' take th' time for all of that now," Ward said, as he reluctantly eased the hammer down on his big .45. "I won't kill them, but I'm gonna' fix them so they won't be anymore threat to us for the rest of our journey home."

While Sina held her gun on the groaning killers, Ward got the picket wire that had served so well and tied each of the cowardly nightriders to a tree. When he had them securely bound he drew his Bowie knife and tested its edge with his callused thumb. Satisfied that it was keen enough for the job, he cut the soles off their boots. He then, with equal satisfaction, cut the brims off their hats.

And while he was still grimly enjoying what he was doing, he removed the saddles and bridles from their horses and fired two shots that started them running back along the trail toward the river. In the meantime, Sina had picked up all of their guns and hurled them in the creek.

"Now," Ward said to the two moaners and the one whimperer—who, of course, was Wes—"you can all walk barefoot to Brushy Creek....I won't take th' time to wait around for it, but I'd love to hear you explain, to whoever finally comes along to cut you loose, how you came to be tied up here with your boot soles cut off and no brims on your hats.

"Chances are they will have seen your horses back along th' trail, and when they see your saddles layin' right over there, you wearin' what's left of your boots and hats, and money still in your pockets, they'll know you haven't been set on by highwaymen.

"I hope a U.S. Marshal is th' first to come along....But come to think about it, with no witness to what happened I doubt if he'd arrest you. But a Marshal could ask some embarrassin' questions and I'll bet he'd send a report to the U.S. Marshal in Brushy Creek...

"You know he'd show it to Bascom, and if that happens I'm sure you can imagine the tongue lashin' you're gonna get when you come limpin' in to face him—with you havin' botched up a chance to blast a Garrison and abuse his wife."

The thought of them abusing Sina made him reach for his gun again. But Sina touched his arm and he let it settle back in its holster.

"Anyway, what ever happens, you listen to this," he went on, "if I ever see one of you swaggerin' around Brushy Creek with a gun on your hip, you'd better start grabbin' for it 'cause I'm gonna t' start goin' for mine!"

Not one of the out-smarted killers uttered a word. They just glared with renewed hatred at the man who had just busted their tails and then tied them to trees with their boot soles cut off!

Sina saw in their glaring eyes the grim promise that they would be looking for another chance. But even though she knew they'd make trouble later, she was still glad that she had stopped Ward from killing them. She had much rather they take their chances with the three camp shooters still alive and looking for vengeance more than ever, than to go through the rest of her life knowing that Ward had killed in cold blood. Her Quaker heart would have shriveled up and died.

While Sina was breaking camp and packing up, Ward sent a chunk flying into the woods with a vicious kick and went stalking down to the creek to get their horses....In all of the campaigns he'd fought during the war, he had never won a battle that had left him feeling so damned unsatisfied!

Chapter 15

Back on the trail with no ambush to worry about, they set themselves a much faster pace for San Antonio. They reached the historic town about noon of the third day after they had thwarted the cowardly attempt on their lives.

Knowing that home was only four hours away, they stopped for just a few minutes to give Sina a quick look at the Alamo. They knew they'd be coming back in a few weeks for the lumber they'd need to start the new house they'd been planning along the way. Sina could then have all the time she wanted to visit the hallowed shrine.

Being one who had risked her life for a cause more than a few times, her indomitable spirit naturally went out to the spirits of the brave men who had died there. Her tears dampened the front of Ward's shirt as he held her close.

An hour later, as they rode southwest out of San Antonio, Sina got her first real look at the wondrous plains she'd heard Ward carry on so much about. She gazed in breathless awe at the endless rolling prairie that stretched in all directions. She immediately fell in love with the awe-inspiring land just as Ward had said she would.

From the high rise where they had stopped to rest for a minute, she could see wild deer by the dozen as well as scores of large cow-like beasts with wide-spreading horns. Ward explained that those were the gone-wild offspring from cattle the Spaniards had brought to the New World three centuries before.

"They will make rich the first few men who can round up two or three thousand and then drive them to the first railhead that comes anywhere close." Ward smiled at the prospect of being one of those hardy men…it was a goal worthy of any man's mettle.

Sina reached for his hand, and in a drawl that mimicked his, she said, "Cowboy, could you teach me how to rope one of them critters?"

Ward leaned over from his saddle and gave her a long loving kiss. He finally settled back in his saddle to gaze once again upon the Irish-Quaker miracle the Lord had fashioned just for him.

Sina smiled back and waited for the words she would never tire of hearing. Ward obliged by saying the words he would never tire of saying: "What a treasure thou art!"

*   *   *

Just before sundown they topped another rise in the wide expanse of grass-covered prairie. Ward reined Buck in and pointed down a long slope that stretched nearly a mile to a tree-lined creek.

Beside the road just before it crossed the creek, there was a ranch house with big cottonwoods standing at the east and west corners. Off to one side was a bunkhouse, and a hundred yards or so down the creek was a barn standing in the middle of a big corral, with a horse trough and a windmill over in one corner completing the scene.

Ward didn't tell her, but Sina guessed, anyway.

"Oh, Ward!" she shrieked with delight, "it's beautiful! I knew it would look just like that. I want us to build one just like it…maybe a little bit bigger."

Ward laughed, and said, "How many kids you figure we're gonna have?"

"Seven or eight," Sina laughed, "a big ranch needs a lot of cowpokes."

On the chance that someone might be looking up the road, Ward stood up in his stirrups and waved his hat. After several big waves he settled back in his saddle and put his hat back on, a bit disappointed at seeing no response.

But before he could say, "I guess they didn't happen to be lookin' this way", two riders bolted from behind the house and came galloping up the road toward them. (He'd find out later that two horses had been saddled and kept standing by from sunup to sundown every day for a week.)

With her auburn hair streaming in the wind and her skirt billowing over her horse's rump, one of the riders had to be his mother. But the other rider was not his daddy even though he was big enough to be. Ward soon saw that the other rider was his little brother Robby all grown up…he'd have to start calling him Rob or Bob.

But where was his Daddy? It was late in the day but not too late for him to still be working on a job in his blacksmith shop.…Ward and Sina lifted their reins, spurred their mounts, and went racing to meet their happy welcomers.

Clods of turf flew as four horses came to stiff-legged halts nose-to-nose in the middle of the road. Ward leaped from his saddle just as his delighted mother and brother were doing. With his arms wrapped around them, and their arms wrapped around him, they rocked and laughed and danced a jubilee right there in the middle of the road!

Finally they paused to catch their breaths and look at each other. Laura's radiant face was still unlined, her blue eyes still just as bright, and her auburn hair still just as thick as it ever was…

Ward knew that he favored his mother, but Robby had grown up looking more and more like their daddy…firm chin, cool level gaze, dark brown hair. He was not quite as tall as Ward but his shoulders were just a broad.…Just the kind of young stalwart Ward had always picked for his cavalry troop. But he was glad Robby had stayed out of the war.

There might not have been enough luck in the family allowance to get them both through all of that hell.

He finally remembered Sina, who was still sitting in her saddle smiling at the joyous family reunion. "Come, Mom, Rob," Ward said, "come meet th' girl of my dreams....And, Mom, just like you are to Daddy, one of the best wives any man ever had. We got married just before we headed home, so there was no time for you to get a letter before the newly weds, themselves, would be arrivin' in th' flesh."

He lifted Sina from her saddle and put her in his mother's waiting arms.

"Ward, she is lovely," Laura said as Sina blushed, "even under a layer of Texas trail dust, I can see that she is a beauty with a lot of fine qualities. How did you ever fool her into marryin' a rough ol' Texas boy like you?"

"Mom," Ward said with mock seriousness, "I have become an officer and a gentleman since you last saw me. Besides that, you didn't do such a bad job raisin' a frontier boy way out here in Texas."

Laura handed Sina over to Rob for a hug and a quick buss on the cheek. When Ward got her back the beam in his eye faded as his thoughts went back to his dad.

"Mom, where's Dad?" he asked.

"Oh, he's at the house," Laura answered, as her face also took on a graver expression, "he's kinda stove up and doesn't get around as well as he used to. He's been thrown from the backs of too many bucking horses...if you look close you can see him sitting on the porch waving his hat."

Ward was relieved at the sight of his daddy waving from a chair on the porch. He responded by taking his hat off and waving it around in big circles, glad to see that his daddy was still alive even though he might not be all that up-and-at-'em anymore.

His mother had not told him in her letters that his daddy was breaking horses. And that started him to wondering what other things she may have kept from him. He had tried not to think about it, but he had known that the Garrison's, being from Illinois, had been marked as "Yankee sympathizers". But he also knew that his family had not expected him to feel sorry for them.

They all mounted up and went galloping down to the house where his smiling daddy was waiting at the head of the steps. As Ward rushed up the steps to greet him, he saw the cane in his hand and how stooped his once robust, square-shouldered father had become. As he was hugging his poor, stove-up daddy, he felt a tear squeezing out…no word was spoken for a long time…

Finally John said, "It's good to have you back home, Son….And who's this pretty young thing you have sweet-talked into comin' to Texas with you?"

Ward introduced Sina and then stepped aside to wipe the tears from his eyes. His mother slipped her arm around him, and whispered, "I couldn't stop him from breaking wild horses…he thought he had to do it to make a living for us after I lost my teaching job."

"Lost your teaching job!" Ward exclaimed, "Mother you didn't tell me…I could have quit the army and come home."

"I couldn't," she whispered back, "I knew we'd get along, somehow. And I didn't want you to come running home like we were giving in. Besides, if you had come home still fit and healthy, you'd have been drafted into the Confederate army."

"Bascom Clark got you fired, didn't he?" Ward guessed, as his father picked up his cane and hobbled down the steps to help Sina and Rob remove saddlebags and bedrolls from the backs of their weary horses.

"Yes," Laura said, "with us being Union sympathizers, he was able to turn all of the townspeople against me. What's more, he bullied everybody into not bringing their horses to John to be shod, or any of their livestock to be doctored. That left him with the only thing he could do for a little income—catch and break wild horses."

"You mean Bascom Clark turned everybody so strong against you, they wouldn't use Dad's services, or let you teach? Before th' war everybody liked th' Garrisons." It was hard for Ward to believe what he was hearing. "Of course," he went on, "it was all because I went to fight on th' Union side."

"No, it wasn't that altogether," Laura wouldn't let him take all the blame, "there are a lot of good folks in Brushy Creek who never felt a lot of sympathy for the South....It was mostly because Bascom hated your daddy for testifying against Wes at his trial.

"To make his wishes clear to everybody, he had several of John's friends beat up and some women insulted. And we are sure he had Harry Wilson's barn burned because he stayed friendly to us longer than anybody....He finally succeeded in bullying everybody into turning against us—even Harry.

"And now that the South has lost the war, Bascom has become even meaner....Not just because the South lost, but because, just before the end, the Confederate Government stopped paying in gold, and started paying him with Confederate money for all the horses and cattle he was selling them. Of course Confederate money is now worthless, and since the officials who had promised payment for goods received are now nowhere to be found, there is nobody he can vent his wrath on except us Brushy Creekers—especially us Garrisons."

"Well," Ward said, "I'm sorry you've been hit with all of that. But now that th' war is over maybe things will settle down and start gettin' back t' normal. 'Specially if we can get a U.S. Marshal in here that Bascom Clark can't lead around by th' nose."

"Yes, that might help," his mother said, "but you watch out. I'm sure Bascom will be looking to give you your comeuppance...you getting to be a Yankee officer and all....I'm afraid he'll be sending two or three of his hired guns to pick a fight with you."

"I'll be careful," Ward promised. He knew it wasn't the right time to tell her about Wes, Tom, and Luther trying to kill him and Sina.

He put on a big smile to restore the homecoming mood as his daddy came hobbling back up the steps with Sina giving him a steadying hand.

"The stubborn old coot won't let me help him like that," Laura whispered through her smile.

"Don't let it bother you, Mother," Ward said, "he's just being 'gallantly polite' to th' newest member of th' family. In time, he'll get back to being his same old self…

"What do you have planned for supper?" he asked, with the same "please-Ma'am-I'm-starvin'" look he had teased his mother with a thousand times.

"Well," his mother teased back just as she had done the same number of times, "I was thinking about some steak and mashed potatoes and some fresh green beans…but if you'd rather have some left-over hog jowl and collard greens…"

"Hush your mouth, woman!" Ward lifted her off her feet and swung her around in a big hug, "come on, let's go to th' kitchen…I'll peel th' taters."

"All right," Laura agreed, "but first, take your things to the back room."

"But mother," Ward said as he put her down, "that would be takin' Rob's room. Sina and I can bed down in th' bunkhouse."

"Ha!" Laura scoffed, "Robby moved to the bunkhouse nearly two years ago…fixed up one of the rooms just like he wanted it, does his own housekeeping, and won't let me come anywhere near it."

"Yeah," Ward said, with an understanding grin, "little Robby is all grown up. And since you and Dad talked him out of joinin' up when he turned seventeen, it's his way of showin' some independence…OK, we'll take it."

Ward peeled the potatoes just as he'd promised, while Sina helped Laura get a fire going in the cook stove and set the table with a clean tablecloth and napkins.

When Ward had peeled the last "tater", he turned to Sina, and said, "Come on. While th' beans and spuds are cookin', let's you and me go down to th' creek and scrub off a few layers of this Texas real estate."

Sina was a little dubious about bathing in the creek before dark. But she relented when she saw the little enclosure John had built in knee-deep water to give Laura some privacy. The water was cold from the springs that fed the little stream, but she endured it with goose bumps and chattering teeth.

"We bathe here until it freezes over every winter, and we don't bathe again 'til th' spring thaw." Ward told Sina a big teasing lie.

"You big spoofer," Sina came back at him, "I know creeks don't freeze over down here, and I've already spotted one of those big oblong tubs hanging by the door of the washhouse. So I know you heat water and bathe in it during the winter months, just like we had to do up in Cairo."

Ward crowded into the little enclosure with Sina, caressed her nude body, kissed her, and said, "If this water wasn't so cold, I'd make love to you right here."

"That's a nice thought," Sina agreed, "and if it was a little darker I'd suggest we get out on the bank."

"Yeah," Ward smiled, "I guess we'll just have to wait 'til we get in bed."

Chapter 16

After supper the men went out on the porch to talk while the women did their talking in the kitchen as they washed and put away the dishes. Of course John wanted to know right off all about the family he'd left behind some twenty-four years before.

"But first, Ward," he said, "let me tell you why I never told you that your real grandmother had died before I left Marlin. That was one of th' reasons I left. I couldn't stand to see her memory so soon sullied by Daddy letting himself fall prey to a fortune-seeking southern wench not half fit to take her place.

"Besides that," he went on, "I wanted you and Rob to grow up thinkin' you had at least one set of grandparents. As you know, your mother's parents died when she was just a young girl. Anyway, I thought I was doin' th' right thing, not thinkin' there'd ever come a time when one of you would get back to Marlin and learn th' truth. I guess it was quite a shock to you...I'm sorry."

"It's all right, Dad, I understand," Ward said, "I was a little shocked when I saw this woman no older than you who was supposed t' be my grandmother. But that was no shock at all compared to some that followed...so get braced for what I have to tell you."

John was certainly not expecting the story to be all that good, but neither was he expecting to hear a story of such treachery, treason, and even murder...murder of his own father!

"Th' murderin' bitch!" he exploded when he heard what Emily had done to his daddy, "I knew she was mean but I never thought she'd go that far. Did you give her what she deserved…a bullet through her black heart?"

"I thought about it, Dad, but I couldn't," Ward said, "but I think bein' reviled by everybody, jailed and stripped of all of her fineries might be a more fitting punishment for her….With her Southern pride crushed and being in prison for life, she is bound to be sufferin' everyday like she was already in hell!"

Ward then went on to tell how he and Sina had watched and waited to foil Emily's treacherous, half-mad brother in his attempt to assassinate Jo. But he didn't tell him that Sina's bullet had actually been the one that finished him off. He left him with the idea that he had done Gideon in all by himself.

Neither did he tell him about Sina coming to warn him that night in the Brass Rail, and how she had shot of one of the killers Emily had sent to get him. Nor did he relate for him any of Sina's daring deeds during the war. All of that could be told later. It would be better to wait and let everybody really get to know her, rather than take a chance on them jumping to some wrong conclusions about his feisty little wife.

Neither was it the right time to tell about him being seduced by Maggie and the two of them being caught with their pants down in the back of Miss Emily's carriage. And of course he said nothing about his near-fatal duel with Evan, Jr., brought on by the shock to his cousin's overweening pride. Those were stories that could wait for an evening when moods were lighter.

But Ward did tell John and Rob about running into the Clark brothers and Luther Tucker in Nacagdoches, and how he and Sina had thwarted their attempt to murder them in their beds four nights later.

John exploded again, and said, "You should have gone ahead and killed them. Odds are, it'll have t' be done sooner or later…

"But," he continued after a moment of thought, "I'm glad you didn't kill them in their helpless condition…I might have gone ahead and done it, but I'm glad you didn't.…I'm hopin' we'll be getting a U.S. Marshal in here who'll make Bascom Clark pull in his horns so there won't have t' be any shootin'."

"I hope so, too, Dad," Ward said. "By th' way," he went on, "I hope Rob has been learnin' how to use a gun, just in case."

"Oh, he has," John assured him, "he soon learned all I could teach him, and I hear him practicin' every few days."

"Good," Ward approved, "and I know you didn't have to tell him that guns are not to be used except when they have to be.…But with th' Clark brothers and Luther Tucker gettin' home any day now, we have to stay ready for anything."

Rob didn't say anything and Ward couldn't see his face in the dark. But he had the sure feeling he could count on him if worse came to worse.

*   *   *

Because they had all sat around talking and sipping John's blackberry wine until midnight, they all slept late the next morning.

As they were finishing up a big, late-morning breakfast, Ward laid his napkin down, and said, "I have a suggestion.…It bein' Saturday, why don't we all go to town? I'll bet there is a dozen things you need, and I want t' see if everything still looks th' same—'specially the schoolhouse, Dad's vet stables and his blacksmith shop."

So an hour later, off to town they went…everybody riding horses except John. Because it had become so hard for him to get up in a saddle, he had hitched up the buckboard. But to head off any pitying thoughts, he had "explained" that it would be needed for hauling back the supplies they'd be buying.

Ward really wanted to see more than the old schoolhouse and his dad's vet pens. He wanted to give some Clark henchman a chance to bully him. If one tried, he figured on making him an "object lesson" for all of the town to see, and for Bascom Clark to hear about.

As Sina looked around at the rough frontier town, she counted about a dozen places of business spaced out along Main Street, and somewhere between twenty-five and thirty houses strung out on each end of it. She noted that no more than a dozen buildings in the whole town had ever been painted.

"Well," Ward observed, as he looked all around, "everything looks about th' same…the schoolhouse could use some paint, and Dad's places will look better when we get all th' weeds cut and all th' cobwebs swept out of th' windows."

"You mean you think folks will start coming back to John?" Laura sounded both surprised and doubtful.

"Well," Ward replied, "he can't expect them t' start comin' back unless he opens up. So why not give them a chance? Anyway, don't you think it might do him good to get back into things instead of hobblin' around th' house all day?"

Laura nodded her head and then said, "But I'm afraid most folks will still be too scared of what Bascom Clark might do…"

"We'll see," Ward said, as everyone dismounted in front of the general store.

As they were stepping up on the sidewalk, Ward suggested, "Why don't you girls get what you need in here, while Rob and I stroll down to th' saloon and wet our whistles. What do you say, Rob? You feel up to a little snort?"

Rob grinned and said he reckoned he did.

Laura frowned, and said, "You boys try to stay out of trouble…I see some Circle C horses tied out front."

"Don't worry, Mom," Ward calmed her fears, "we won't stir up any trouble....When Dad gets here, tell him where we are in case he wants t' come and have a sip with us."

Laura said all right, but she looked after them with worry lines creasing her brow...Sina's brow was showing some worry lines, too.

As the saloon doors were swinging to behind them, they paused to look around for a moment. Ward spotted four men sitting at a table over near the far wall. He was sure they were Circle C hands who had ridden into town on the horses tied out front. He noticed that one of them was wearing a faded confederate shirt.

With long, self-assured strides the two brothers walked up to the bar, pushed their hats back, put their elbows on the polished slab of mahogany and planted two big boots on the brass rail....The Garrison brothers had boldly thrown down the gauntlet to any man in the room who wanted to challenge their claim to three yards of drinking space at the bar!

Ward smiled and said, "Hello, Mr. Garner. Remember me?...I had my first drink in here 'bout four years ago."

"Well," the dour-faced barkeep said without a smile or any sign of welcome, "I can't say that I remember you havin' your first drink in here, but I know who you are...what'll you have?"

"Well," Ward said, "since this will be Rob's first drink, let us have some of your best stuff...somethin' smooth that'll go down real easy."

Barkeep Garner grunted, turned to select a bottle from the shelf under the big mirror, and then turned back to uncork and pour...

But Ward said, "Hold it just a minute...let's put that bottle back and pull the cork on one that's never been opened."

Barman Garner hesitated with the cork in his hand, but under Ward's steady gaze he finally grumbled a mild protest and did as Ward had suggested.

With the undiluted stuff from the new bottle in their glasses, the Garrison brothers were saluting each other and taking their first sips, when one of the Circle C hands said in a voice heavily slurred with liquor, "Hey, Yank, wuz you at Vicksburg?"

Ward had been keeping an eye on the four Clark C henchmen by way of the big mirror behind the bar. The one who had asked the provoking question was the one wearing the faded confederate shirt.

Ward turned around slow, and said, "Yeah, I was at Vicksburg."

"Yeah," the ex-reb snarled, "then you wuz one of them dirty blue bellies who poisoned th' water that made ever'body sick...I watched women and little kids die!"

"No," Ward coolly denied his accusation, "we didn't poison th' water. You Rebs kept drawin' all th' wells dry fightin' th' fires that got started. With no water left in th' wells, everybody had to drink filthy branch water. That's what made everybody sick."

"If there's anything I hate more than an out-and-out Yankee, it's a smart-assed, lyin' Yankee!" the ex-reb shouted.

Spurred by the bitter dregs of defeat that he could still taste in his mouth, he shoved his chair back, lunged to his feet and started groping for his gun.

"Watch th' barkeep!" Ward told Rob as he drew his gun and fired in one smooth motion.

The ex-reb's hand was just closing around the butt of his gun when Ward's slug knocked it out of his hand and spun the empty holster around to his backside.

"Easy, boys," he warned the other Circle C hands as they started coming up out of their chairs, "if I have to go up against all three of you at th' same time, I can't afford t' take chances shootin' at guns...I'll have t' shoot at bigger targets."

They all dropped back into their seats and raised their hands. As the ex-reb was raisin' his he kept looking at his numb right hand as if he wasn't sure it was still attached to his arm.

With every hand high in the air, Ward glanced at Rob. He smiled when he saw him standing steady as a seasoned trooper with his gun leveled at the uneasy barkeep's big belly.

"All right," Ward said to the four Circle C hands, "stand up and unbuckle your gun belts and drop 'em on th' floor.

"Now," he said, when the last gun hit the floor, "go out and get on your horses and hit th' road home."

As the four Clark riders started moving to the door. Sina burst into the room with her finger tight on the trigger of her little .38. Laura was right behind her with her double-barreled derringer cocked and ready, and John was right behind Laura with his old muzzle-loader drawn and the hammer fully cocked.

"It's all right everybody," Ward yelled, as five pairs of hands reached even higher, "everything is well in hand…these boys were just leavin'."

All of the just-arrived Garrisons eased off on their triggers and stepped aside to let the four Circle C hands make their exits. Ward followed them out to their horses and checked to make sure none of them was carrying an extra gun in his saddlebag. When he finally stepped back and motioned with his gun, the four Clark hands mounted up and rode out of town without a word of back talk.

After looking into the muzzles of five cocked guns with a Garrison looking down each barrel, they were no doubt glad to be making tracks out of town.

When Ward got back inside the saloon, he found Rob still standing at the bar with his gun still leveled at Bob Garner's big paunch.

"OK Rob," he smiled, "I think you can put your gun away now…you did good. Let me show you what you kept him from gettin' his hands on."

He stepped behind the bar, reached down and pulled out an ugly looking double-barreled shotgun. He broke it open, pulled the two shells out, and said, "Hm-m-m, buckshot.…Mr. Garner, when you fire this thing at a man, you really mean t' hurt him, don't you?"

"Well," the surly barman said, "a man has to protect his property…but I wouldn't have used it on you or your brother."

"I wouldn't count on that," John spoke up, "you boys did right to watch him. Everybody knows Bascom Clark owns a big interest in this place, and that puts Bob Garner in his camp. In any trouble with th' Clarks, you'd do well to keep an eye on him."

"We will, Dad," Ward assured him, "and you might keep that in mind, too, Mr. Garner."

With the shotgun still in his hand, Ward turned at the door, and said, "I'll be leavin' your gun outside leanin' against th' wall…but don't be too quick about comin' to get it."

As they were all walking back to the general store, Ward noticed the glum looks, and said, "Everybody stop looking so glum…lift up your heads and smile.…We have just sent a message to Bascom Clark tellin' him that the Garrisons aren't goin' to be pushed around any more!"

As they walked on toward the store with every chin up and a smile on every face, Ward told John and the two women what had happened.

"Yeah," John said, "I hear that ex-reb lived in Louisiana. But he couldn't go back to face everybody at home after Vicksburg fell, even though the Yanks told him and all of the rebs to go home and forget about the war. Instead of goin' home, he came out here where he wouldn't have to face his family and neighbors.…He had done way too much braggin' about how he and the other rebs were goin' t' whip th' pants off them Yankees.…They say that every time he gets to drinking, he starts talkin' about Vicksburg and how they would've won if th' Yanks hadn't poisoned all th' wells."

"Yeah," Ward said, "I guess th' truth is a pill that's just too bitter for him to swallow."

There were several of their former friends in the store when the Garrisons came walking in. They had all heard the shot in the saloon, and had seen the four Circle C riders leaving town at the point of four Garrison guns…some of them smiled at a Garrison for the first time in three years.

Laura and Sina went to the piece-goods counter where they'd been when they heard the alarming shot. John and Ward went over to the hardware section.

Some five or ten minutes later, as Ward was paying Tom Logan for some horseshoes, he suddenly realized that Rob hadn't followed him and his dad to the hardware section. He looked all around and finally spotted him in a far corner talking to someone. He couldn't see who he was talking to until he took a step back. He almost dropped his horseshoes when he saw it was Diann Clark, Bascom Clark's daughter!

"Well, I'll be…" he said to himself, "I remember now…they were sweet on each other in school. It looks like they still are…but I'll bet ol' Bascom doesn't know it."

He looked around the store again and finally spotted the Mexican woman who used to meet Diann after school to take her home. Apparently Bascom still wouldn't let Diann go anywhere unchaperoned, but now, as a grown up girl wanting to keep her romance alive, she was conspiring with her motherly chaperon to slip out now and then to meet Rob in some secluded glen, or in the store as he had just seen.

If Bascom ever found out Ward knew there'd be hell to pay!

While everybody else was mounting up for the ride home, Ward stepped up on the buckboard and seated himself beside his daddy.…Earlier that morning as they'd all come riding into town, not one person had spoken or even looked their way. But now, as they were leaving town, nearly everyone along both sides of the street looked up and spoke as they passed by.

John looked at his son with a lot of pride showing, and said, "I guess th' word has already got around that we are fightin' back, and we ain't gonna be bullied, anymore."

"I guess so, Dad," Ward smiled, "and I wish you'd think about openin' up your businesses again. You can hire a man to help out, and I'll be around to help some, too."

John squared up his shoulders, and said, "I'll start on it in th' mornin'…I'm tired of sittin' around th' house all day, anyhow."

Ward was pleased that his daddy was already showing signs of his old self.

"There's somethin' else I want to talk to you about," he said, "Mom told me in one of her letters that your Uncle Brad had died. And with Aunt Selma having already passed on, leavin' them childless, he had willed all of his property to you. I'd like to buy some of it for Sina and me to build a house on and start a ranch…a section or two down th' creek from you and Mom." John's Uncle Bart had come to San Antonio as a land speculator in '37 and had done quite well for himself.

"Well," John said, "I reckon that can be arranged. There are six sections down that way—three for you and three for Rob. All they'll cost you is the transfer-of-deed fee…there is plenty more land down that way you can buy cheap."

"Thank you, Dad," Ward accepted the gift and the suggestion, "now tell me more about all those longhorns wandering around down there just beggin' t' be rounded up and driven to market."

"They are there all right," John assured him, "that was beef from one of them you ate last night."

"It was?" Ward said, "well it sure chewed easy and tasted mighty good."

"It came from one Rob roped nearly a month ago. We penned it up and fed it some grain…we managed to sell what we figured we couldn't use."

"Hey, that was good timin' for Sina and me," Ward laughed.

"Well," John drawled, "we've got a couple more fattenin' up in th' pen. But now that you are home you'll have to pitch in and help slaughter th' next one."

"Well," Ward imitated his daddy's drawl, "I reckon I ain't forgot how…bein' in th' cavalry made it easy to round up stray cows…"

Chapter 17

The next morning when everyone had finished their breakfast, Ward looked around the table, and asked, "How do you all feel about us dressin' up and goin' to church?"

"Well, I guess we could," Laura sounded a little doubtful, "it's been more than a year since we've been....We weren't welcomed with open arms..."

"Well, Mom," Ward said, as he glanced at his daddy, "let's give 'em another chance...folks might not be so unfriendly today."

So they all started getting ready. The men shined their boots and picked out their best ties, while the women heated the smoothing irons and start pressing pleats, cuffs and collars.

Rob saddled a horse to ride, then helped Ward put another seat on the buckboard so he and Sina could ride along with John and Laura. Ward didn't wear his gun, but he hid it under a sack in the bottom of the buckboard. He didn't know it but Sina had slipped her little .38 in her purse.

A crowd was already gathering around the church when they arrived. Most of the men were gathering in one group, while most of the women were getting together in another one. John led his sons over to the men's group while Laura led Sina over to where the women were gathering.

Everybody in the men's group stopped talking as the Garrison men approached…nobody made a move until Harry Wilson stepped forward, stuck his hand out and said, "Howdy, John. I'm glad t' see you."

John took Harry's hand, and said, "Howdy, Harry. Glad to see you, too. You remember Ward, and of course you know Rob."

Harry wrung Ward's hand, and said, "Glad to see you back, Ward."

"I'm glad to be back, Mr. Wilson," Ward smiled, as Harry turned to shake Rob's hand.

The ice was broken and everybody in the group shook hands with them…Tom Logan, the storekeeper, Jake Walker, the town cobbler, Hank Porter, the barber, and all the others.

Nothing was said about the war or Bascom Clark. And nothing was said about the Garrisons hazing four Circle C hands out of town.…But everybody was more at ease around a Garrison than they'd been in years.

Ward glanced over to where the women were all gathered in their group. They were all laughing and carrying on with Laura and Sina as if the last four years had never come and gone. But he knew that Sundays at church usually brought out the best in folks…things could be a lot different on Monday.

He looked around for Homer Bisbee, and saw that he had just arrived and was just then stepping down from his buggy at the back of the church. He expected Reverend Bisbee to come join Harry and the other men for handshakes all around, but he didn't. Without even taking the time to dust himself off, he picked up his Bible and hymn book, went up the back steps and right on in the church.

Ward thought maybe there was something in the church he had to do before services got started. His not coming over to shake hands and welcome some members of his flock may not have had anything to do with the Garrisons being present. Even though Homer was married to Bascom's niece, he didn't want to accuse him of being partial. But on the other hand, no other preacher had ever married into a family that was lorded over like Bascom Clark's.

He began to wonder if Bascom was going to be there. He glanced at his watch and saw that it was only three minutes until starting time. That started him to wondering why the church bell hadn't been rung twenty minutes ago to remind everybody it was the Lord's day. A little while later he found out why.

Everybody finally started going inside and taking their seats. But when John started leading his family to the rickety back pew where they'd had to sit the last time they were there, Harry Wilson took John's arm and shepherded the Garrisons to the front pew they'd sat on every Sunday before the war.

There were tears on Laura's cheeks as John took his seat beside her.…There were some tears on some other cheeks in the congregation, too.

After a few minutes, Ward took another peek at his watch and saw that it was well past time for church to start. But nobody seemed to be getting the least bit impatient, especially not Reverend Bisbee.

Finally, twenty minutes later, Ward heard the clomp-clomp of hooves, the creak of harnesses, and then the sounds of a rig being brought to a halt in the churchyard. There was a brief stir in the congregation and Reverend Bisbee "came to attention" in his chair. Ward naturally guessed that the stir in the congregation and Homer's "coming to attention" had something to do with who was arriving in the rig.

He was not really surprised when he looked over his shoulder and saw Bascom, his wife, Ursula, and his daughter, Diann, coming down the aisle. He hadn't thought much about the vacant pew across the aisle from where the Garrisons were sitting, but when the Clarks "took possession of it" he knew why it had remained unoccupied.

He was a little surprised to see Mrs. Clark out in public on her crutch…a sorry substitute for the leg she had lost as a young girl. Laura told him later that Ursula had started attending church much more often, two, three years back when Bascom was reaching his pinnacle of power and domination.

Laura also told him at that later time why the church bell hadn't been tolled to "announce" that services would be starting in twenty minutes. Bascom had told Homer to stop ringing it…church service would not begin until he got there no matter what time that might be.

While everybody was finding the right page in their songbooks and were getting to their feet to sing the first hymn, Ward saw ol' Rob sneak a look at Diann. He didn't blame him for his interest in her. She had turned out to be a fine looking girl…blue eyes, long chestnut hair, and a blouse full of nice bosoms.

When the song was finished, and while everybody was sitting back down, he was not too surprised when he saw Diann sneak a look at Rob.

What a rocky romance that could turn out to be! Ward wondered again if he should talk to Rob. He immediately decided not to. If he were in Rob's place he wouldn't listen, either. When the time came for them to make their move he'd take on the whole Clark Clan by himself, just like he knew Rob would.

Reverend Bisbee preached what was probably the worst sermon of his career. He had to correct himself three times in reading his text. And when he started preaching he kept on misquoting the text he'd had so much trouble reading.

He had no doubt heard about the gunplay in the saloon, and he could very well be worried about gunplay and bloodshed right there in the Church! —Or maybe he just hadn't prepared the right kind of sermon for the tension-filled situation he was in.

Anyway, he finally gave up, closed his Bible, and asked everybody to stand for the closing hymn. When the last words of the hymn had been sung, he muttered the benediction and headed for the back door as if he was expecting a gunfight to break out at any second.

Ward soon saw that another rule had been laid down since the last time he had attended the Brushy Creek Church. When he got up to leave he saw that nobody else had made a move toward the door. Everyone was waiting until the "Sovereign Clarks" had made their way up the aisle, through the door and down the steps.

Bascom had issued the rule on the pretext that someone might bump into Ursula and cause her to fall. Ward immediately wondered why the Clarks didn't use the back door as Homer had just done. But then he realized that—from the autocratic Bascom's point of view—back doors were for nobodies, not for a "Lord of the Realm".

Ward approached the fancy rig just as Bascom was settling himself on its plushy seat.

"Mr. Clark. Miz Clark," he spoke politely, "I have some news for you. I saw Tom and Wes and Luther Tucker back up th' trail a few days ago. They dropped in on my wife and me rather unexpected one mornin' just before daylight. But as they came galloping into our camp they all fell off their horses. Oh, they weren't hurt bad, but they didn't feel like gettin' up or doin' much talkin' for awhile...

"We left them sittin' in restful positions with their backs against trees....I'm sure they all got to feelin' better and soon got back on th' trail home. But since their horses had run off it'll take them awhile longer t' get here. I know this has not been th' best of news, but it beats hearin' nothin' at all, wouldn't you say?

"And while we are talkin'," Ward went on, "I have a proposition for you....I'll forget that your sons and hired gunman so rudely disturbed our sleep, if you'll snub them up a little tighter, pull in your horns and try to be a little more neighborly."

Bascom's face flushed red under his bristling beard, and he bellowed, "Neighborly! You talk about bein' neighborly when you may have left my sons to die somewhere back on th' trail!...I'll wait 'til they get home—if they ever do—before I do any talkin' about bein' neighborly!"

"I guess that's fair enough," Ward agreed.

When Bascom lashed his team into a sudden start, Ward had to jerk his foot back to keep his toes from being run over!

The old range lord had left Ward with the sure feeling that things were going to get worse before they got better.

Chapter 18

That afternoon Ward and Sina rode down along the creek to look for the just-right place to build their house. Ward already had a site in mind but he hadn't told Sina anything about it. He just rode along behind her as they approached it, wondering if she would see the almost perfect location for a ranch house, barn, and corral…

Just when she was about to ride past it, she reined her horse in and shrieked, "Ward! This is it! Just the place I had in mind!"

"Yeah, I think it's a good place, too," Ward agreed, with a smug look on his face.

Sina maneuvered her horse in close and pinched a big welt on his side.

"You had already picked this spot, hadn't you?" she said, "and you were just waiting to see if I'd ride right past it…well, Mr. Smarty Pants I didn't, so when do we start building?"

"Well," Ward drawled, as he rubbed the welt on his side, "we can start drawin' plans as soon as we get back to the house. When we've finally settled on one we like, we'll hire a carpenter and let him work up a list of materials. We'll then go to San Antone, haul a load back and start buildin.'"

Sina got down from her horse and said, "Oh, Ward, I'm so excited.…Let's put the kitchen right here looking down toward the creek; the living room here so we can look out on that breathtaking vista to the south; the bedrooms over here to catch the night breezes....And that spring down there, we can wall up around it, put a pipe in it, and pump water right into the kitchen and bathroom."

"Hey," Ward smiled, "that's exactly the way I had it figured...but let's add a wide veranda on th' side of th' house that'll be shaded by those two big cottonwoods."

Ward finally got Sina away from their home-site-to-be and took her on a ride to see some of their soon-to-be ranch. He led her through grass that was belly high to their horses and stayed green the year round; under live oak trees that spread their branches over half an acre to shade cattle while they chewed their cuds; then back along the spring-fed creek that could water every cow in the county and keep right on flowing through the driest of summers.

As they were riding back along the creek, he showed her an Indian camp-site that had been used by various tribes in their seasonal wanderings for hundreds of years.

"Are there some Indians still around here?" she asked, as she looked all around.

"Well," Ward said, "Dad tells me that bands of Comaches are seen pretty often, but there have been no attacks on settlers in a long time. Which of course doesn't mean that we can start lettin' our guard down....With buffalo gettin' scarce up to th' north, more of them could start rangin' down this way to kill mavericks for their jerky, and of course they never pass up a chance to steal a horse."

Sina sighed resignedly and wagged her head...did there have to be a serpent in every Eden?

*   *   *

After two days of working around the kitchen table—relieved at intervals by rides to the building site to make sure they'd be arranging rooms just right to get the most out of the setting they had chosen—

they had a rough plan ready. They turned it over to Les Morgan the next morning for him to work up the list of materials they'd need to get started.

While Les was doing that, Ward and Sina pitched in to help John and Rob get the blacksmith shop, the vet office and the stalls all ready for business. But truth be told, Sina kept Ward out in the corral a lot of the time, teaching her how to use a rope. After two days of roping fence posts, she had insisted on him bringing in a gentle milk cow so she could practice on "the real thing".

One afternoon while Ward was trying to teach her how to rope the docile old bossy from the back of a horse, they heard John calling them from inside his office.

"There's some folks here to see you," John said, as Ward opened the door.

Stepping inside from out of the bright sun blurred their vision for a moment, but then Sina recognized Jo and Ward recognized Josh.

"Jo! Josh!" they both greeted their friends at the same time.

"What a nice surprise!" Ward said, as he wrung Josh's hand while Sina was hugging Jo.

Ward stood back, looked from one to the other, and said, "But how...what...are you two...?"

They both laughed and Josh said, "Yassuh, we's married...fo' days after you two left Cairo...we tried to catch you, but you was movin' too fast."

"That's great," Ward slapped his leg and laughed, "two good friends meetin' and marryin' and then comin' t' Brushy Creek....But, hey, I'm forgettin' you don't know Sina...Josh, this is Sina...Sina, this is Josh. He was the farrier for my cavalry troop...th' best horse shoein' man in the army...

"I have a brother around here somewhere, and a mom back at th' house. Speakin' of house, come on let's go there so you can get something to eat and rest up...you passed the Garrison place just before you crossed th' creek."

They met Rob at the hitching rack outside. His eyes got a little wide when he saw black folks for the first time, but then he smiled, stuck his hand out and gave each of them a warm Texas handshake.

When Josh and Jo and everybody else had eaten, and while they were all sitting out on the porch letting their supper settle, Josh told their story...

The folks who'd been so good to him in Indianapolis had lost nearly everything in a land deal. and couldn't keep him on after the war.

He remembered what Ward had said about him coming to Brushy Creek, so he had saddled up his horse and headed for Texas. He had stopped in Marlin to ask about Ward and was told that he might find him at Clancy's Inn in Cairo.

But of course he'd gotten there too late. But being late had proved to be the best thing that had ever happened to him, because that's where he met Jo.

They had hit it off from the moment Jo had served him his first bowl of Mrs. McGee's Irish stew. But it had taken him three days to talk her into going to Texas with him. If she hadn't already known and trusted "Miss Sina" and "Mistah Wahd" so much, she might never have agreed to go back south even if it was "way off to the west".

He turned to Ward and said, "Jo told me 'bout the trouble you had with your step-grandmomma, and how you fine'ly got everything all straightened out for th' Garrison family...and then how you and Miss Sina saved her life. We both owe you folks a mighty big debt and we is here to pay some on it."

"Ah," Ward brushed his talk of debt aside, "there's no debt to be paid. Without Jo's help we'd have never nailed Miss Emily. We're just glad she was quick to throw that salt shaker....By th' way," he turned to Jo, "I suppose you gave some testimony before you left?"

"Yessuh," Jo replied in her velvety voice, "I give th' District Attorney what they calls a...dep...a deposition."

"OK," Ward said, "we just want t' be sure Emily doesn't go unpunished for what she's done."

"Oh, I'm sho she want," Josh shook his head, "what she'd done was already comin' out in th' papahs...

"Speakin' of somebody bein' mean," Josh continued, "three jaspers tried to steal our hosses 'bout twenty miles up th' trail from San Antone. I'm purty sho I winged one of them, but they got away."

"Did you find any tracks?" Ward asked.

"Yassuh, I sho did...I showed Jo....They was all barefoot! If I hadn't got a good look at one of 'em and saw he was white, I'd a thought they was Indians."

Ward grunted and said, "Yeah, they were white all right....They were th' same jaspers who jumped me and Sina. But we were ready for 'em and spoiled their fun....'Shoulda killed them, but instead of doin' that we ran their horses off and cut th' soles off their boots....I'm sorry to have to say it, but I'm sure we'll be havin' problems with them again because they are from the Clark spread on the other side of town. But don't go thinkin' you have brought us trouble—things couldn't be any worse between us and th' Clircle C than they already are."

"All right, Cap'n, if you say so," Josh replied. Then after a moment he chuckled, and said, "Thas good...runnin' their hosses off and cuttin' th' soles off their boots so they'd have t' walk home barefoot."

"Yeah," Ward grinned, "I'm glad you ran 'em off before they got away with **your** horses...I'm especially glad that we threw their guns in th' creek where they couldn't find them."

"Yassuh," Josh nodded with a grave expression on his face, "I'm glad for that, too."

"Now," Ward said, as he looked at John for his approval, "there are two extra rooms in th' bunkhouse that we can fix up for you newlyweds to live in until you can get a place of your own....So come on, we'll carry your stuff down there and get you set up...tomorrow you can start shoein' horses."

Chapter 19

While Les was working up the list of materials he'd need in building their house, Ward busied himself around the vet pens helping his dad. While he worked he kept his eyes peeled for Wes, Tom, and Luther. After two days he'd seen no sign of them. But that evening at the saloon he heard they'd been seen just after noon bypassing town to the north.

He figured they had bought the horses they'd been riding in San Antonio on Bascom's credit. They had probably bought themselves some new boots and hats, too. He alerted his family that the Clark Clan was back to "full strength" again, and would very likely be looking to start trouble…

He would've given a ten dollar gold piece to have heard the tongue lashing the old Mexican-American War veteran had laid on his two "undistinguished" sons. He heard later that their "welcome" home had gone exactly the way he had figured…

*   *   *

Expecting to be welcomed back with open arms, Tom and Wes had rushed in to be warmly greeted. But instead finding Bascom waiting with open arms, they found him sitting behind his big, intimidating desk with his beard bristling and Ursula standing beside him on her one good leg like a surly stork.

"Well," Bascom growled when his two inept sons had come to an uncertain halt before him. "Some fine sons you are!...You botch a good chance to blast a Garrison, and let him get home to brag in my face about leavin' you tied to trees!"

"But, Pa," Wes whined, "how was we t' know he would have wire strung up all around his camp at just the right height t' catch a feller right under his chin?"

"Ain't you ever heard of doin' some scoutin' before you attack?" the old veteran shouted. "Three of you against one man and a mewling woman and you let yourselves be taken like two puny peons! If you can't be Clark men," he went on, while his neck veins swelled alarmingly, "I'll just put you on th' payroll as stable cleaners and manure spreaders! So get out of here and start earnin' your keep!"

With hangdog looks on their faces they turned to leave. But before they could get to the door, Bascom added a strong admonition.

"Don't go tryin'", he sternly warned them, "t' think up somethin' t' do to th' Garrisons to impress me. You'd just botch th' job, and wind up in jail...

"We could be gettin' a Yankee Marshal in Brushy Creek any day now, and we don't want to do anything until I find out if he's a man I can deal with....So before you do anything to the Garrisons, check with me first...comprende?"

"Yes, Pa," the boys mumbled as Wes meekly opened the door and then eased it to behind them.

"Mama's boys." Bascom growled at Ursula, as the door closed behind the two sons they hadn't seen in nearly four years.

"They are your boys, too," Ursula curtly reminded him, "who else would get in bed with a one-legged woman!"

Chapter 20

During the next month, Ward divided his time between helping Les at the house site and lending his dad a hand in the vet pens. The Garrisons had all gone to church on the next two Sundays, but the Clarks had not been in attendance either time.

Some of the Circle C hands had been in town two or three times every week, all of them on every occasion behaving like little cherub-faced altar boys. But nobody in town had seen hide or hair of Tom, Wes or Luther Tucker since they had come home. Ward wondered if the talk he'd had with Bascom could have helped that much. He doubted it, but time would tell...

When another week went by with no trouble from the Clarks, Ward began to feel like he was sitting on a keg full of unstable blasting powder....When trouble finally came, he couldn't believe that anyone, not even the Clarks, could stoop so low!

One Tuesday morning while he and Sina were helping Les and his hired hand nail up some boards on their new house, they heard a horse coming down the road at a fast gallop. A few moments later they were surprised to see that it was Laura on the back of the galloping horse. She reined the horse in beside them, and with her eyes flashing anger she told them that Josh had just been arrested and thrown in jail!

"They are saying he stole a Circle C horse!" she added, "John and Rob are at the jail seeing that nothing worse happens to him...Jo is there, too, of course."

Ward and Sina dropped their hammers, mounted up, and went galloping back up the road with Laura.

Ward knew it was a frame-up. They all knew it and could testify that Josh had been at home all night. But they also knew the Clarks had no intention of letting the case come to a matter of them having to prove their charge in court. They had no intention of letting Josh be brought to trial. They aimed to hang him for winging a Clark, and send a message to the Garrisons that something just as bad or worse could happen to them.

They all rode straight to the jail where they dismounted with a grimness of purpose that warned Abel Gunderson to mind his manners and keep his big butt out of their way.

Abel, the jailer and a Clark henchman, didn't try to stop them, but he did grumble something about "too many folks crowdin' his jail cryin' over a nigger horse thief". They ignored his grumbling and went straight to the cell where Josh was locked up...Sina went to Jo, Ward went to Josh.

"Buck up, Josh," Ward told him, "nothin' worse is gonna happen, and we'll have you out of here as soon as we can get a judge to set bail."

Josh looked up and said, "Thank you, Cap'n...you know I didn't do it."

John took Ward outside and told him what had happened.

"Abel Gunderson and Barney Hatcher were waitin' at the shop when me and Josh got there this mornin'," he began. "Accordin' to Abel, Barney had told him that the horse he rode in from the Circle C last night was missin' this mornin'. And when he went lookin' around town for him, he just happened to look in the corral behind th' blacksmith shop, and lo and behold, there was his horse!

"I walked around and looked," John continued, "and there was a Circle C horse in th' corral, all right, and there was a strange saddle hanging on the rack in the shed. Right away I point out that nobody in his right mind would steal a horse, and then leave him in th' corral where he worked. Barney and Abel both shrugged, and Abel said, 'Who can account for what a dumb nigger will do'?

"I insisted they leave the horse and saddle right where they were until we could get some things sorted out. Which of course was all right with them, since they think the more folks who see the horse and saddle in th' corral and shed, the stronger their case against Josh will be."

Ward knew that Barney lived in town but worked out at the Circle C. Bascom let him ride one of his horses to the ranch and back every day....

He motioned for John and Rob to come with him down the sidewalk a ways. When they were beyond the range of Abel's well-practiced, eavesdropping ears, Ward said, "Dad, Rob, we all know what the Clark's are up to....They aim to hang Josh, but of course we don't aim to let them...we'll stop them with bullets if we have to...but I have an idea that might save some bloodshed...

"I read somewhere awhile back about police using bloodhounds to track down criminals. We of course don't have any such dog, but we can "let it be known" that the police in San Antonio have one, and that we are goin' t' have him brought down here to sniff that saddle, and then track the man who last handled it right to his house.

"So let's start spreadin' the word and see who comes sneaking around tryin' to get at that saddle to wipe it clean....Dad," he went on, "after dark this evening, get Harry Wilson, or some other impartial witness, to hide in th' shop with you so you can nab whoever comes in and starts wipin' on that saddle.

"Meanwhile, when Wes or whoever, comes leadin' a mob of Circle C hands into town with th' notion of lynchin' Josh, Rob and I with Sina and Mom, will be waitin' behind th' saloon to discourage any such notion....You can bet they'll be stoppin' there to get themselves liquored up…I think there's a good chance th' framer will show up to wipe that saddle before we have to call their hand."

"Well," his father said, "I think your trick has a good chance of workin'. But on th' other hand, if there are too many of them, and they should come in before dark.…"

"Dad," Ward said, "you should know they're not going to hang a man in broad open daylight. And you know how well you taught me and Rob to shoot.…You know Mom doesn't miss with a shotgun or rifle, and I guarantee you Sina can clip a cat's whiskers at twenty paces. What's more, before he gets liquored up, you know Wes Clark can be faced down by an old granny woman with a pop gun."

John reckoned that Wes might be faced down that easy, but he knew there were gun hands at the Circle C that Charlo the Breed couldn't face down.

But he didn't say anymore. He knew the Clarks had to be stopped before the citizens of Brushy Creek could ever reclaim their town, and feel secure in their homes. He was proud that his sons were stepping forward to lead the fight against the high-handed Clarks and their hired guns.

"Dad," Ward said, "you go to th' saloon and start spreadin' the word about this new way of catchin' criminals, and how we aim to use it to catch whoever it was that framed Josh. We want barkeep Bob Garner—Bascom's number one spy in town—to be th' first to hear th' story.

"Rob you go tell th' story at the barber shop, while I go back to th' jail and tell it to Abel Gunderson…we'll see who starts a rider to the Circle C first—Abel or Bob Garner."

Ward put his hand on his brother's shoulder and they exchanged long, serious looks. No word was spoken, but the look they gave each other was all that was needed. Ward knew that Rob was no "little brother" anymore, and could be relied on as surely as any man who ever sat a saddle in his troop.

He went back in the jail to tell Abel how they aimed to prove Josh's innocence by bringing in a dog to sniff the saddle, and then track the last man who had touched it right to his house. Abel tried to pretend he was not the least bit interested but Ward saw him turn pale around his "gills".

He then walked back to the cell where Laura and Sina were still trying to reassure Josh and Jo. He suggested they take turns staying at the jail to keep Josh company and see that he was not abused. He promised to hang around close and drop in every few minutes the rest of the day. The women agreed and of course Jo wanted to take the first turn.

As Ward, Sina, and Laura were leaving, Ward paused to whisper in Abel's ear, "If anything happens to that man or his wife, you won't live to see another day!"

When he had caught up with the two women, he let them in on his ploy to nab the Clark toady who'd put the horse in Josh's corral. He then suggested that they all go eat lunch at the hotel, and spread the word there about a dog that could track criminals to their doorsteps.

In less than twenty minutes he spotted a Clark toady headed toward the Circle C. Five minutes later he spotted a another one pounding leather in the same direction. He was pleased to see that whoever had been paid, or had been ordered to set Josh up, would soon be getting the word about the "new way" of catching criminals.

Harry Wilson had agreed to join John in the blacksmith shop to nab whoever tried to sneak in and wipe their scent off the saddle. It was now just a matter of being patient for a few hours and keeping Josh's spirits up.

Finally, as darkness shrouded the little town under clouds that blotted out the moon and every star, the solemn-faced Garrisons all looked to their guns, put extra shells in their pockets, and started taking their positions....John at the blacksmith shop with Harry, every other Garrison behind the saloon, where they'd fidget and wait and hope they'd hear John's signal that the framer had been caught before Bascom's hanging crew arrived.

They all knew that this could be a crucial battle in the war to wrest control of Brushy Creek away from the old range lord...

Ward kept hoping along with the others that they'd hear John's whistle. With a trusted citizen as a supporting witness, the frame up would be exposed, Abel would have to let Josh go free and everybody could breath big sighs of relief and go home. But just before midnight when he heard riders approaching on the far end of Main Street, he knew that Josh's lynching would have to be stopped the hard way.

He heard the self-appointed purveyors of justice dismount in front of the saloon, then a few moments later their boots clomping on the saloon floor as they all swaggered up to the bar.

He squeezed everyone's hand in his, and then led them through the back door into the storeroom that opened off the barroom. From there, Ward counted ten men crowded around the bar, gulping their shots of nerve boosting straight whiskey. He recognized Wes and Luther Tucker in the light that was much dimmer than usual. He guessed that Bob Garner had lit only a few lamps so the faces of men bent on murder, would be harder to recognize by a late carousing patron who might later be called as a witness.

Ward knew that Luther was the most dangerous one of the lot. Besides being Bascom's paid killer, he knew that Luther had a score to settle with him after being so badly bested back on the trail. He was sure the proud gunman was eager to recapture the self-image he'd lost.

He turned to his mother, and whispered, "OK, Mother, you stay here and guard our backs. Rob you slip through th' door and step to th' left, while I move straight ahead. Sina you move over to the near end of th' bar to make sure Bob Garner doesn't get to his shotgun...and you be sure to duck behind th' bar if any shootin' starts."

The four of them were in position before any member of the whiskey-guzzling lynch mob took notice...

"Well, Wes and Luther," Ward got their instant attention, "I see you are both wearin' guns, and I'm sure you both know what that means."

Wes didn't make a move, but Luther immediately eased his right hand into position over his gun, and said, "Well, Yankee Boy, you think you are ready for a showdown, huh? I was hopin' you'd show up...you know I owe you."

Luther Tucker had killed his first man when he was sixteen, up in Kansas during the pro-slavery versus anti-slavery battles in that blood-drenched state. Since he had filed that first notch on the butt of his gun, he had sent hot, death-dealing slugs slamming into the chests of at least ten other men...

He still remembered how their faces had gone blank when his slugs had hit them. He smiled as the memory boosted his confidence. To further bolster his confidence he was sure that he had dropped at least four men who were faster with a gun than this Yankee soldier-boy who was used to drawing his gun from a wrong-way holster.

He felt his thumb curl around the hammer as his fingers closed around the well-worn butt of his .44....He felt the familiar heft of the gun and the hammer click on full cock as the barrel cleared leather...it was one of the fastest draws he'd ever made.

But his finger went numb before he could pull the trigger. His chest exploded with pain, and his knees started buckling. As he was slumping to the floor he felt his face going blank just like all of the faces on the men he'd gunned down!

Ward had bested Luther by a fraction of a second...only a fragment of time, but it meant the difference between life in the sunshine and death in a cold, dark grave.

As Luther was slumping to the floor, Ward heard the roar of Rob's gun. He glanced to his right just in time to see a man stagger back with a bullet in his shoulder. He had tried to sneak his gun out at the same time Luther was drawing his...Rob had been too quick for him, too.

The aspiring young gunman had had the foolish notion of killing Rob while Luther was dispatching Ward. That would have entitled him to share honors with Luther and put him on the road to fame. But it hadn't worked out that way. All he had gotten for his sneaky effort was a bullet-shattered shoulder, and a painful end to his dream.

Ward next thought of Sina, but when he glanced her way he saw that she had things well in hand. Bob Garner was up on his toes reaching for the ceiling and begging, "Don't shoot! Don't shoot! Ease up on that trigger!"

"All right, Wes," Ward said, as he stared into the eyes of the cowardly camp shooter, "now it's your turn....You remember what I told you to expect if I ever again saw you carryin' a gun. I spared your worthless life back on th' trail even after you tried to kill me and my wife, but I'm not goin' to this time...but I will give you a fightin' chance. I'll holster my gun and let you go for yours first."

Ward dropped his gun back in its holster, and got ready to draw the instant Wes touched his gun. But the little coward's hand didn't go anywhere near his gun. Both of his hands started groping for the ceiling as the blood drained from his face. His mouth started working as if he was trying to say something, but before any words came out, his knees buckled and he fell in the offal he was vomiting on the floor!

While Wes' disillusioned henchmen were gazing in disbelief at their big-talking leader, the saloon doors flew open and Barney Hatcher came stumbling into the room.

"Well," John said, as he gave Barney another prod in the back with the barrel of his gun, "I see I'm a little late, but here is th' lowdown little varmit who took Bascom's money to frame Josh. Maybe what's left of this lynch mob would like to hang him—one of the real criminals in this case."

He then looked with puzzlement from Luther to Wes to the young dreamer with a bloody shoulder. Finally he said, "I heard only two shots...?"

"Luther and the young bucko in th' chair are the only ones who got shot," Ward told him, "Wes fainted rather than go for his gun."

"Too bad," John grunted, "but I see you got the most dangerous one…

"OK," he went on, "since you seem to have everything under control here, Harry and me will march Barney down to th' jail and make Abel turn Josh loose…

"Hey, Wife!" he whooped, when Laura appeared in the storeroom door, "glad to see you are all right…but you be careful with that old scatter gun…you know it has a hair trigger."

"Yeah," Laura smiled, "I sneezed the other day and it went off in the closet!"

John laughed as he and Harry grabbed Barney by his arms and hustled him out the door.

"Hey, Dad," Ward shouted after him, "untie these jaspers' horses and fire your gun behind them…I think they need t' take a long walk 'to think upon their folly', as some bard once wrote…

"Now," he went on, as he turned his attention back to the remaining members of the lynch mob, "all of you would-be 'dispensers of justice' drop your gun belts right where you stand. Then when you get your cock robin leader back on his feet, all of you hit th' road back to the Circle C."

Bob Garner poured a bucket of water on Wes and they finally got him up on his rubbery legs. Two of his henchmen half-dragged, half-carried him out the door while two other men did the same for the glory-seeking young waddy whose dream had ended with a bullet-shattered shoulder. Brushy Creek had no doctor, but Ward figured Bascom's Mexican vet could dig th' bullet out and rub some horse liniment on his wound.

After once again taking Bob Garner's shotgun from under the bar and unloading it, Ward took Sina in his loving arms and held her tight. It was then Laura's turn to be hugged, and then Rob's.

As they were leaving the saloon to go hug Josh and Jo, Ward hurled Bob Garner's shotgun way out in the weeds. They all knew they had won an important battle. But they also knew that the war with Bascom Clark and his Circle C gang was far from being over…

Chapter 21

In another week Ward and Sina's dream house was finished. Since the shootout in the saloon, they had slept at the unfinished house to guard against a sneaky attempt to burn it in retaliation for having exposed the Clark's vicious scheme to hang Josh.

Sina was of course eager to get their new house furnished....She'd bought a few pieces of furniture from Tom Logan's limited inventory, but she and Ward had bought the rest of it on two delightful overnight trips to the big furniture store in San Antonio. (Where Sina finally got to take all the time she wanted to visit the Alamo and commiserate with the spirits of the heroes who had fallen there.)

After Laura and Jo, along with some helpful friends, had spent a week helping Sina make curtains, bedspreads, rugs, tablecloths and doilies, the house, as they say, had finally taken on the look of a home.

Josh now had all the work he could do...shoeing horses, mending harnesses and saddles, and repairing wagons, buckboards and buggies. And John had to hire a hand to help him in his rejuvenated vet business.

With the house finished and the sulking Clarks "licking their wounds" and re-grouping, Ward and Rob busied themselves rounding up longhorns.

To hold the semi-wild critters they were collecting, they put a fence across the open end of a box canyon, and then put a gate in the fence. They then added "wings" to each end of their fence to "funnel" the critters to the gate and on into the big natural corral. They collected eighty of the longhorned critters the first week, hired two vaqueros the next week, and burned the Bar G brand on the right rumps of two hundred more.

"That is money on th' hoof," Ward assured Sina, "except they'll have to be trail-herded to Kansas to turn 'em into cash....When we get two or three thousand rounded up, we'll start our big drive...meanwhile, I'm gonna buy a blooded bull, pick out th' beefiest lookin' cows, and start breedin' better stock."

When there was no retaliation of any kind from the Clarks in the month following the shootout, Ward wondered if it might be because of what he'd heard....He'd heard that the Circle C was busy rounding up mavericks on the west side of Brushy Creek, and were putting a big herd together for a trail drive of their own. That might be so, but until Bascom "had him in his pocket", Ward figured the period of peacefulness could be chalked up to the arrival of a U.S. Marshal two weeks after the shootout.

Whatever was in the wind, he'd soon find out. Juan Vasquez, one of the vaqueros he'd hired, had a cousin who rode for the Circle C and they got together every Saturday night for a friendly drink in the saloon. He'd be getting another report from Juan in a few days as to what Bascom might be mulling around in his devious mind.

Thomas Archibald Gilchrist, the new U.S. Marshal, was from Missouri where he had supported the Union side during the war. For his loyalty in a divided state, he had been rewarded with an appointment to U.S. Deputy Marshal. He was strictly a political type with no hard experience behind a badge or toting a gun.

Ward doubted if Tom Gilchrist alone would ever put much fear of the law into Bascom and his hard-bitten, scofflaw crew. But just his presence behind a U.S. Deputy's badge, might put the old range boss on notice that his highhanded flouting of the law could bring an unfriendly troop of Union cavalry down on his neck. But Union troops or not, Ward doubted that Bascom and his scofflaws had backed off for good. Bascom had probably ordered everyone to lie low until he had made "some arraignments" with the new marshal.

Brushy Creek's new marshal had arrived on the first stagecoach from San Antonio. It had been the first run for the new line that had prom- ised twice-a-week service between Brushy Creek and the Alamo City. This new service had of course given everybody in the town at the end of the road the feeling that they were now on the map, and more in touch with the rest of the country.

Ward rode into town on Wednesday of the third week of Brushy Creek's new link to the outside world, to visit with his dad and pick up a few things for Sina.

When he saw a crowd gathered in front of the hotel, he figured every- body was waiting for the new coach to arrive. Since he hadn't seen it up close, himself, he decided to stop and join the crowd.

He had tied Buck's reins to the hitching rail, and was just turning around, when new stagecoach coach come wheeling in with the driver hauling on the reins and hollerin' "Whoa! Hosses, Whoa!".

The four big horses were reined in "with great effort", and the big coach was braked to a rocking halt in a swirl of dust in front of the hotel…a big show for the benefit of the frontier crowd that had gath- ered to watch.

Crowds had started gathering on every "coach" day, not only to see the show the drivers put on, but also to see who might be coming to their end-of-the-world town. Being a little curious, himself, Ward moved around to a spot that would give him a better look at who might be getting off…he figured it would have to be a census taker, a land speculator, or a new Indian agent.

The driver and the mustachioed feller who'd ridden shotgun began handing down all of the boxes and suit cases, and Bill Fletcher, the hotelkeeper and the town's self-appointed greeter, came rushing out to open the coach door.

When Bill had opened it wide and stepped back, a murmur of a-a-h's went up from the wide-eyed onlookers. The admiring murmurs continued as Bill put out his hand to help a very smartly dressed young woman step down from the coach. When she finally had her stylishly shod feet firmly on the ground, she lifted her veil to reveal her lovely face.

Ward's knees went limp! He had to grab hold of a hitching post to steady himself! The smartly dressed young woman, whose good looks had made everybody go "a-a-h", was Maggie Carson!

He knew he should pull his hat down over his face and quietly slip away. But he couldn't stop staring at her and that was probably why it was so easy for Maggie to spot him in the milling crowd.

She dazzled him with a big smile, and held his gaze with her lovely eyes for a long moment. But then, lest she focus too much unwanted attention on poor, dumbfounded Ward, she turned to share her dazzling smile with the whole crowd.

She finally held up a white-gloved hand to quiet the stir around her and to get everybody's attention. When everybody had quieted down, she said, "My name is Margaret Carson, and I am a Doctor of Medicine. I have come to set up practice here in Brushy Creek to give you the medical service you deserve but have never had.

"I studied medicine four years at the Illinois Medical School, and then practiced with my father for two years. I am fully qualified to deliver babies, set broken bones, and treat gunshot wounds—to say nothing of headaches, stomach aches, fevers, and women's complaints…I'll be available day or night, rain or shine."

There were a few unapproving scowls, but her announcement went over well with most of those who'd heard her.

In all of the hustle and bustle of unloading her baggage and getting it moved into the hotel by a dozen eager-to-help males, Ward managed to get close enough to whisper in her ear, "Meet me in th' veterinarian's office up the street in one hour."

He slumped in a chair at the vet office, told his daddy the dilemma he was in, and asked if he could borrow his office for a few minutes. John said of course and then asked if there was anything else he could do. — Like kidnap the brassy wench, haul her off to Mexico and sell her into slavery!

Ward said thanks but he'd try to handle the touchy situation, himself.

It didn't seem at all strange to folks who, a little while later, saw Doctor Maggie Carson stroll down to the veterinarian's office and go right in.

After all, they were both in the doctoring and healing business, and should get to know each other in order to be able to share the benefits of new-found medical discoveries in each of their fields of practice. And what other person in town could one of them call on for consultative help on tough cases that were not responding to standard treatment?

When Doctor Maggie walked in, Ward looked up from behind his daddy's big desk and asked right off, "Are you really a doctor? And if you are, with all of the other doctor-less towns on th' frontier, why did you have t' pick Brushy Creek?"

Could he ever forget her green eyes and all of her shiny black hair? To say nothing of her warm lovely legs.

"Well," Maggie purred, as she glided around the end of the desk, "even though one knows only one or two persons in a strange town, he or she doesn't feel so much like a stranger when they get there. And to answer your other question: Yes, I am a doctor, fully qualified to practice medicine in every state."

"Then why," Ward asked, "didn't you stay in Marlin and take over your daddy's practice?"

"Daddy wasn't ready to retire," Maggie shrugged, as she continued to glide around the desk, "and besides, I had a good reason for wanting to get out of Marlin."

"What was that?" Ward asked as he slipped out of his chair and retreated a step.

"I'm pregnant," she replied, with her eyes locked on his.

"You mean you finally got Evan to show some passion?…Then why didn't you just get married, and stay in Marlin as his wife…?"

"It's not Evan's," Maggie set him straight, "the baby is yours!"

"What!" Ward moaned, as he fell back another step, "you mean that one time…!"

"That's all it takes," Dr. Maggie assured him, as she moved in closer and started fiddling with a button on his shirt.

"But…but you're not showin'," Ward protested as he pushed her hands away and moved back another step.

"It's been only four months, and I'm wearing loose clothes…"

"But what about Evan? Surely you and him had…uh, er…well you know what I mean."

"Yes, I know what you mean…but no, we never did what getting babies require. I tried my best to seduce him every night for a week after I knew you'd got me pregnant, but he wouldn't have me…not after his precious ego had been so terribly shattered when he saw me with you."

"The vain bastard," Ward cussed him, "if he was here I'd shoot him again right where I already shot him once!"

"Yeah," Maggie smiled, "it amuses me, the targets you pick…but you might as well have killed him for all the good it did me for you to spare his life."

"I'm sorry, Maggie…but you must know that I… I'm…"

"Yes, I know you are married to Sina…but I have to find out if you want to stay married to her under these new circumstances."

"Maggie, again I'll say I'm sorry. But I do want to stay married to Sina. And if you do anything more to…"

"Don't worry about it, Ward," Maggie said, as she turned away and went back to the other side of the desk, "now that I'm sure about how you feel, I won't cause any more trouble."

"Thank you," Ward said, as he took his hat off and mopped his brow, "but what are you goin' t' tell folks about you bein' pregnant?"

"Oh," Maggie shrugged, "I'll just say my husband died of his war wounds just before I left Marlin."

"Maggie," Ward double-checked, "are you sure that baby is mine? You are a passion 'rousin' woman, and I'm sure you have been, er…pursued by other men."

"No," Maggie firmly denied, "there was nobody before you for nearly a year, and nobody since."

Ward knew she was telling the truth.

"All right," he said, "but don't let it slip that it's mine."

"You mean don't tell Sina? Oh, I'll guard well against that." Maggie made her words an oath by solemnly raising her right hand.

"That wasn't exactly what I had in mind," Ward said, "I aim t' tell her, myself, th' minute I get home.…She guessed right off why Evan and me had our duel…

"I may be sleepin' in th' barn for a few nights but I can handle that.…This is what I had in mind: If th' whole town was to find out that I fathered your baby, Sina would be awfully bad hurt—'specially since she is beginning to doubt if she can have a baby of her own."

"Ward," Maggie said, "I understand perfectly, and I promise that I will never tell a soul. If it is at all possible, I want to be friends with you and Sina."

"All right," Ward said as he reached for his hat, "but don't expect to be seein' much of me for a few days."

He followed Maggie to the door and as she was stepping outside, he said, "I'm sure you'll do well here…Brushy Creek needs a doctor."

"Will you call me if you get sick?" Maggie asked, with an eyebrow raised over a teasing smile.

"I sure will," Ward quickly assured her.

Chapter 22

Ward told Sina just as he had told Maggie he would.

Storm flags started flying in her lovely cheeks, but they soon subsided as her Quaker upbringing cooled her Irish temper. She knew that nothing could ever break the bond between her and Ward...but with all of her forgiving Quaker teachings, she did not so quickly forgive Maggie.

She knew that Maggie had used her pregnancy to try to take Ward away from her. That was a sneaky thing to do after she and Ward were already married, especially since Maggie was just as much to blame as Ward...just as much to blame? Ha! Even more!

She hoped that she and Ward could soon have a baby of their own...they could start working on it again just as soon as he had served his time in the barn.

*   *   *

Maggie got a chance to prove her medical prowess the very next day after she arrived in Brushy Creek...

Harry Wilson's hired hand came careening into town in a buckboard just after sunrise to tell her that Harry had met with foul play and needed a doctor quick! She of course grabbed her medicine bag and climbed aboard the buckboard to be rushed to her first patient in the Brushy Creek area.

Laura heard about the new doctor being rushed out to the Wilson place, and rode down to tell Ward....

Sure that the Clarks had had something to do with it, he saddled Buck and rode straight out to Harry's place. He found Harry lying on his bed with Maggie working over him.

"He has a broken arm and a broken rib," Dr. Maggie Carson gave him her diagnosis, "but he'll recover in good time."

"What happened, Mr. Wilson," Ward asked.

"Two nightriders rode me down," he said, barely above a whisper, "they was tryin' t' burn my barn agin!"

"Did you see who it was?" Ward was already pretty sure.

"It was dark so I can't say for sure. But from the way they sat their saddles they looked like Wes Clark and Jesse Wiggins."

"That figures," Ward growled, "I'm gonna kill that weasel Wes th' next time he crosses my path!...maybe that low-life Jesse Wiggins, too!"

But Harry raised his hand and said, "No, not on my word alone...I couldn't swear on a Bible it was them."

Ward could see that Maggie had done a professional job in splinting Harry's arm and binding his rib. But he was curious about something he saw.

"What's that for?" he asked, as he pointed to a tube stuck through a hole in Harry's side.

"Well," Maggie informed him, "the broken rib nicked a lung. I inserted the tube to drain off the fluids to keep it from collapsing. I think it can be removed tomorrow, and if he is kept in bed for a few days, he'll pull through just fine...I'll stay with him 'til noon."

As far as Ward was concerned Maggie had passed her first test with flying colors. But for her sake as well as Harry's, he hoped her patient survived. As for Wes Clark and Jesse Wiggins?...if Harry died—maybe even if he didn't—they were on borrowed time. He clinched his jaw as the tips of his fingers brushed the butt of his gun...enough was damn well enough!

But two days later, thanks to Maggie's good doctoring, Harry was sitting up in bed hollering for more grub. Two days later, he was walking around town telling everybody how glad they ought to be to have Dr. Maggie doing her doctoring in Brushy Creek.

"They would have never got me to San Antonio alive," he correctly asserted, "with that broke rib gouging into my lung, I would have drowned in my own blood."

Ward was glad for Harry and Maggie, but Wes Clark and Jesse Wiggins had better stay well out of his sight.

Maggie's next case was delivering a baby. Instead of Maria Sanchez, the local midwife being called into attendance, Maggie was called and she made a completely professional, uneventful delivery.

She did, however, do one thing different from what most doctors or midwives did. She scrubbed her hands with soap and warm water before she touched her patient.…It had taken her awhile, but back in Marlin she had even got her daddy in the habit of doing it.

The next day Maggie went to have a talk with Maria. She suggested that they team up and work together in delivering the next two or three 'muchachoes' that arrived in town. The wise old sonora agreed. She knew that she could very well learn some things from this college educated doctor…things that might help her better serve Mexican women who would never think of sending for a gringo doctor. And, quien sabe, the city-born, city-trained lady doctor might learn a trick or two from her.

*   *   *

One morning a week or so later, Hamer Smith limped into Maggie's office with his chronic case of lumbago acting up again.

"…Had it as long as I can remember…even as a kid," he told Maggie, "I've tried every liniment I can find but it ain't helped."

Maggie had seen Hamer come limping in.…

"Has your right leg ever been broken?" she asked.

When Hamer said no, she said, "Stand over there so I can get a good look at you.

"Now," she said, "put your feet together and stand up as straight as you can."

She saw Hamer's trouble at once. His right leg was shorter than his left one and that was throwing his spine and hips out of line.

She put a thin book under his right foot, and said "Now, Mr. Smith, stand relaxed for a minute and then tell me how you feel."

Hamer stood at ease for a minute and then cautiously waggled his shoulders and then his hips. After twisting to his left, then to his right, he bent over and then squatted down. When he straightened up, he said, "Well, I' be doggoned…it feels better!"

Maggie measured the thickness of the book, and said, "Go to the shoe shop and have the cobbler build up the sole of your right shoe a half inch. It'll take awhile for you to get used to it but I'm sure it will relieve your lumbago."

A week later, instead of him hobbling around town grunting and groaning, Hamer was walking straight up, smiling at everybody and singing the praises of Brushy Creek's new doctor just as loudly as Harry had.

*   *   *

Maggie's pregnancy had been showing for the last two or three weeks. And when folks heard the "poor widow's" sad story of having lost her war-wounded husband, they wagged their heads in pity. —Not just for the poor woman who'd lost her dear husband, but even more for the poor infant that would come into a cruel, pitiless world with no father to protect it "from the buffetings it would suffer on the rough sea of life".

Ward's face took on a pained look every time he heard such talk. But Maggie just smiled and told everybody not to worry…some good man would be coming along.…

One quiet morning when Maggie was returning from her pregnant-woman walk, a Circle C rig pulled up in front of the hotel where she had her office. The old driver got down, and said, "Miz Clark is hurtin' real bad and wants you to come doctor her."

Maggie said, "Of course," and immediately went for her little black bag.

The old driver helped her get aboard the fancy surrey and she settled herself on one of its soft, plushy seats. She had heard some disturbing things about the Clarks and the Circle C, but doctors were sworn to go where and when they were called…

She had been quietly enjoying the sweeping vistas that met her eyes from every rise in the road, but she had not been prepared for what she saw when the old driver stopped the surrey on top of a high rise in the prairie. The proud old manservant wanted her to have a good look at the breathtaking scene that stretched to the horizon before them.

She followed the sweep of the old servants arm as if he was drawing back a big curtain, and beheld a ranching empire that must've been as big as some counties!…A world of its own lying in a wide green valley that stretched to the south and north as far as she could see. As her dazzled gaze came back to the rambling hacienda that sprawled over half an acre, the old servant didn't have to tell her that she was looking at the main headquarters of the giant Circle C ranch.

Just beyond the grand hacienda that would've done any Old Spanish Don proud, there were three bunkhouses—each of which could house more than a score of cowhands. Flanking the three bunkhouses was a huge kitchen along with a mess hall that could easily seat a hundred men. Beyond those buildings were barns, stables, corrals, and all the mills and workshops needed to service the vast ranch and keep it throbbing with life.

The old manservant pointed out the racetrack that could just be seen in the distance. It was the track on which horses selected as candidates for breeding had to first prove their speed and stamina. Only the fastest over the long course were allowed to propagate their kind in the breeding pens.

Just beyond the track, huddled in a bend of the river—the life blood of it all—was a cluster of adobe huts that housed the crop tenders.…The planters, the pruners, the pickers who tended the rich fields that produced the foodstuffs needed to feed everybody from the Lord of it all down to the humblest peon.

Maggie could understand how easy it would be for a man who owned all of what she was seeing to become imperious and dictatorial.…A lord so high and mighty he couldn't tolerate anyone who tried to say him nay, and was capable of eliminating any man who got in his way, or refused to bend his knee!

When they arrived at the grand hacienda, the old manservant helped her down from the surrey and led her across the wide veranda to the big front door. A maid met them there to usher Maggie into Bascom's inter sanctum and leave her standing all alone in his "august" presence.

As she waited for her presence to be acknowledged, she took a quick look around and found herself standing in the middle of an outsized room that looked more like a museum commemorating Bascom's proud participation in the Mexican-American War, than it did a place for greeting callers and doing business.

On the wall behind Bascom was a huge life-size battle-scene painting with smaller paintings arranged on both sides…one of them being a portrait of the old veteran himself in his Major's uniform.…Trophy cases filled with army weapons—pistols, rifles, swords, bayonets, Bowie knives—stood around the walls at precise intervals, with flags and pennants on standards in between. It was an impressive collection of wartime memorabilia, all capped off by a full-sized howitzer hulking in a corner over to her left.

Maggie wondered if the old shell launcher and all of the other weapons were just for show, or if they had been collected in response to a problem Bascom might be having with paranoiac anxieties?

With her doctor's eye for details, she noted that every weapon in the old veteran's arsenal was completely free of rust and dust. Could that mean, she speculated, that he was keeping every weapon ready for instant use in case of a sudden uprising of his peons…?

Ah, well, Maggie sloughed it off, if that was what it took to ease the old man's anxieties and make him feel more secure…

Without making any move to get to his feet, Bascom finally acknowledged her presence with an impatient glance at her and her little black bag. With a grunt that clearly showed his disdain for a woman who called herself a doctor, he pointed to a door off to his left that had been sized to the same proportions as the other parts of the outsized room.

Maggie smiled and nodded then turned to follow the young maid to the door the old range boss had so brusquely pointed out. The maid opened the door, and Maggie stepped into a meagerly furnished bedroom where a woman—presumably Mrs. Clark—was lying on a very plain bed.

Maggie immediately wondered if the old range boss—who had spent a fortune on his "security-blanket" weapons—had adamantly refused to let his wife buy the furnishings and decorations that the austere room cried out for, or if Mrs. Clark just didn't have any appreciation for finer things.

The maid "announced" Maggie and then quietly withdrew to a far corner of the room.

Ursula glanced up at Maggie and motioned for her to sit in the chair at the side of the bed. When she had removed her hat and coat, and had seated herself in the chair that looked as if it had been borrowed from the bunkhouse, Ursula said, "I hear you know something about doctoring."

Maggie smiled, and said, "Yes, Ma'am, I think I do.…What seems to be your trouble, Mrs. Clark?"

Ursula put her hand to her head and moaned, "It's this pain in my head…it's there nearly all the time but today it is worse."

Dr. Maggie Carson reached for Ursula's wrist and began checking her pulse. While she counted, she studied her patient's face. What she saw reflected in the poor woman's face and eyes was enough to give a Mexican burro a headache!…Extreme tenseness, suppressed anger, resentment, frustration, shattered dreams, haunting fears….

The poor woman! With all of the wealth she had around her—maids to wait on her hand and foot, never needing to turn her hand—how had she come to such a sorry state?

Maggie went on to give Ursula a complete bedside examination: Eyes, ears, tongue, throat, chest, stomach. She found no alarming symptoms anywhere, but she wondered about the severe tautness that she could feel in her patient's abdominal muscles. Maggie saw that it was impossible for Ursula to completely relax them, even when she asked her to try.

When Maggie finally sat back to look once again into her patient's eyes, Ursula looked away and said, "Doctor, it's not just the pain in my head…I also have these terrible pains in my leg."

"Oh," Maggie said, "then let's take a look at it." She pulled the covers back and was startled to see that her patient had only one leg!

"I'm sorry," Maggie murmured as she began examining the poor woman's remaining leg.

"It's not that leg, Doctor," Ursula moaned, "it's the one that's been cut off!"

Maggie stopped her examination and sat back in her chair. She hadn't been prepared for that, but she was not too shocked by Ursula's words. She had heard of the "phantom pain" that some amputees suffered…it had become all too common during the war. But she knew from her studies that there was no prognosis except drugs to dull the senses, and trying to explain to the patient that it was all in their mind.

"Have you been taking anything for the pain?" Maggie asked.

"No," Ursula replied, "nothing except a small glass of whiskey now and then and it doesn't help much."

Maggie nodded, and said, "I'm going to give you something that will relieve your pain, relax you, and let you get some sleep." She had learned early in her practice that positive assurance made the medicines doctors gave their patients much more effective.

She gave Ursula two big spoonfuls of laudanum, and then sat back to see if it would be enough to relax her and put her to sleep. She doubted that trying to explain would do any good but she might try sometime later. After about twenty minutes Maggie was pleased to see Ursula relax and start breathing normal in deep, blessed sleep.

She picked up her medicine bag and motioned for the maid. "I'm leaving this bottle of medicine," she instructed. "Keep it from her except when the pain gets real bad, then give her a big spoonful."

The maid took the bottle and asked, "Did she tell you about the pain she has in her leg?"

Maggie smiled sympathetically and said, "You mean the one that's missing? Yes, she told me about it. This medicine will help her forget her missing leg."

The maid looked at Maggie with widening eyes, and said, "But, Doctor, her leg is not really missing. She wouldn't let it be buried. It's wrapped up like a mummy, and she keeps it in a box under her bed!"

"Are you sure?" Maggie gasped.

"Yes," the maid said, "I have seen her holding it in her arms, moaning and talking to it!"

"Oh, my God," Maggie groaned, "how long has this been going on?"

The girl shrugged, and said, "The old maid before me said she saw her do it on her wedding day...she couldn't stop grieving when her sweetheart wouldn't marry her after she lost her leg.

"From what I hear," the too-talkative maid continued, "on top of losing her leg and then her sweetheart, Mrs. Clark has had a very hard life. She wasn't even allowed to be a real mother to her two sons.

"…Saying that he wanted his sons to grow up to be real men instead of mamma's boys who'd been coddled and pampered by their mother, Mr. Clark took them away to be suckled by young mothers who'd just been freshened by having babies of their own. Mrs. Clark got to hold them and play with them—against Mr. Clark's orders—only when he was away…

"What love she had left by the time little Diann came along, had been smothered so long I guess it just couldn't be brought back to life. Anyway, little Diann was raised almost completely by a Mexican woman."

"So," Maggie said, "poor Mrs. Clark has never had anyone to share her pain, or to help her forget even a little of her disappointment and grief. And she tries to console herself by 'nursing' and rocking in her arms, her mummified leg!"

How the poor woman was holding on to what sanity she still had, was beyond any explanation Maggie could think of—much less come up with a cure for the poor woman's immediate plight!

When she looked back at the pathetic figure on the bed with the covers lying flat where her lost leg ought to be, she was glad to see that Ursula was still resting easy under the influence of the double dose of laudanum.…She knew that the woeful, misused woman was beyond Earthly help.

The maid closed the door behind Maggie and she went to report her findings—some of them, anyway—to her patient's husband. Bascom showed no interest at all and impassively dismissed her with only a mild complaint for the double fee that she was charging him.

On the way back to town, Maggie sat on the back seat of the surrey and wondered if the self-centered Bascom would have kept Ursula around had she proved to be barren. She quickly concluded that he would have kicked her out and searched the whole frontier for another white woman to "incubate" and bear his sons. She was quite sure that

Major Bascom would never have settled for four or five half-breed sons running around his domain calling him Daddy!

She finally put a stop to her musings and asked the old driver to go slower over the rough places...she didn't want to risk losing the precious baby she was carrying.

Chapter 23

After having corralled more than four hundred longhorns, Ward and Rob were obliged to range farther and farther south to find more of the free-for-the-taking, gone-wild Spanish cattle.

Prompted by their daddy's suggestion, they bought some salt blocks and placed them in good locations to entice the critters into closer, easier-to-catch places. Places where they'd be easier to rope or drive into the winged opening to their natural corral. With less hard riding, and the hazardous business of roping a thousand pounds of dynamite with horns and slashing hooves, they corralled sixty head the next day.

Now that her house was more or less in order (did any woman ever get her house fixed exactly as she wanted it?) Sina quite often went on maverick roundups with them. Ward wouldn't let her throw a rope on a bull, not even a full-grown cow, but he did let her lasso some of the horn-less yearlings…which she did when she could urge her horse get in close enough.

Roping mavericks and pounding a saddle all day was hard work. But it left one with the exhilarating feeling of having braved the dangers of doing a hazardous but exciting job. And after a quick bath in the creek and a bowl of beans and bacon, restful sleep came without the aid of a sleeping pill. It was work that tested one's mettle, but those who could handle it could sit a little taller in their saddles.

Sometimes in their search for the wandering longhorns, they'd spot a Circle C rider on the west side of Brushy Creek. One day they spotted two Clark riders watering their horses at the stream that more or less divided the territory between the Circle C and the Bar G. But no Clark rider had ever been seen roping a maverick on the east side of the creek.

Probably, Ward guessed, because there were more of them to be rounded up in the huge valley west of the creek....Anyway, he didn't see any need to start worrying since there were still more on the east side than he and Rob could ever round up....And it was worth noting that the primitive critters seemed to instinctively wander from one side of the creek to the other, to let grazed-over grasses recover...which was another factor that pretty well eliminated any need for worry.

One evening as they were riding home after a long day in the saddle, Sina complained of a pain in her side. Ward asked if she had been thrown from her horse and had "forgotten" to tell him about it. She denied that she had and told him not to worry...she'd had pains in her side before and they had always gone away in a day or two.

After supper, which Sina hardly touched, instead of letting her go bathe in the creek, Ward fixed a bath for her in the house and put her to bed early.

But she was restless all through the night, and by the next morning her face was flushed with fever. She had to admit that she was having more pain in her side than she'd ever had.

Ward immediately went to find Juan and they quickly hitched a team to the buckboard.

"Juan," Ward said when they had buckled the last strap, "don't spare the horses on th' way there, but hold them in check on th' way back...Dr. Maggie is pregnant and mustn't be bounced around."

When Ward got back in the house and told Sina that he had sent for the doctor, she gave him a half-teasing smile, and said, "Don't you know that she could overdose me with something and leave you unprotected from her wanton desires."

"Sina, Honey," Ward said in a mildly scolding tone, "doctors swear oaths…and you know I would never let her come anywhere near you if I thought she'd harm you."

Sina smiled again, and said, "Well, I guess we have no choice. In fact, I'm beginning to think that us folks in Brushy Creek are lucky to have her." Ward gave his beloved Sina an understanding nod and then kissed her feverish brow.

Fortunately Maggie had not started out on her regular morning walk, and Juan was back in record time—with Laura as well as the doctor.

Doctor Maggie Carson greeted Ward with a brief, "Good morning" and went straight to Sina's bedside.…

"Hi," she said, "I've been wanting to tell you how much I admire you for all you did during the war…helping the slaves and all.

"But most of all, for what you did there at the last in helping Ward expose the infamous Miss Emily. And Jo has told me how you also helped Ward protect her against Emily's brutish brother…Everybody should have a friend like you . Now let's see what your trouble is."

With tears in her eyes, Sina took Maggie's hand and held it for a long moment between hers.

It took only a minute for Maggie to determine the cause of Sina's pain. She sat back in her chair, looked first at Ward then Laura, and then back to Sina.

"It's your appendix," she said, "it is badly inflamed and must be taken out before it ruptures. I'll have to operate immediately…Ward, go put some water on to boil so I can sterilize my instruments."

Sina started to protest but sensing her fears, Maggie said, "Sina, Honey, you won't feel a thing…I have some chloroform, and with Ward and Mrs. Garrison here to help, the three of us can handle everything nicely and you'll come through it just fine."

As Ward was filling the teakettle he offered up the most sincere prayer he had prayed since the last Confederate stronghold he had charged. He knew that very few people survived an appendicitis operation. But he also knew that no one survived a ruptured appendix. He saw his mother turn to one side, clasp her hands in front of her breast, and offer up a fervent prayer of her own.

As gently as it could be done, they carried Sina to the kitchen table. And when everything was ready, Maggie dampened a clean washcloth with chloroform, held it over Sina's mouth and nose and told her to take a few easy breaths. She did, and was soon asleep.

Maggie then handed the cloth and the bottle of chloroform to Ward, and said, "Keep it damp, and when I nod put it back over her nose and mouth."

Then with Laura standing by, Maggie made an incision in exactly the right place and quickly located the inflamed appendix.

While helping to restrain wounded soldiers Ward had watched army surgeons at work....Never had he seen one with hands as skillful as Maggie's. Not once did she make a wrong move and she nodded for more chloroform at exactly the right time every time...not too much, not too little.

With the touch of an angel, Maggie removed the useless vestige. She then deftly cleaned, folded and sutured the stub from which it had come. With that done, she quickly closed the incision with nine neat stitches and the job was done.

Dr. Margaret Carson then gave her patient a shot that would dull the pain, and put her in a deep sleep for a few hours.

She knew the battle was not yet won....She had been as careful as she could be, but infection could still set in. The next twenty-four hours would determine whether Sina lived or died.

They carried her back to the bed, and before the shot had taken full effect, she opened her lovely eyes, and murmured, "Is it all over?"

"Yes," Ward whispered back to her, "and you are goin' t' be just fine."

"Thank you, Doctor," Sina mumbled, as her eyes closed in sleep.

"Don't let her have any food or water when she wakes up," Dr. Maggie ordered. "You can wet her lips every five minutes with a wet cloth, but that's all…I'll be back this afternoon."

Ward and Laura took turns sitting by Sina's bed. She was quiet for several hours, but as the shot wore off she became restless, and her fever began to rise. They bathed her face with a cool damp cloth and murmured loving assurances.…

She woke up in the afternoon, but she didn't recognize either of them. She looked around fearfully, began to thrash about, and then started begging for water. They wet her lips with a damp cloth, but she was so thirsty she grabbed the cloth and tried to squeeze more water into her mouth. Restraining her, and having to forcibly remove the cloth from her hand, made them feel mean and cruel, but they did as Maggie had ordered. From then on each time they dampened Sina's lips, her hands were firmly but lovingly held.

When Maggie arrived about mid-afternoon she saw that Sina's fever was dangerously high. She gave her another shot to calm her, then wet a cloth with alcohol and applied it lightly all over her body. Sina finally calmed down and dropped off to sleep.

She woke up again just before midnight and it was the same thing all over again. Her fever soared, she begged for water and had to be restrained each time they wet her lips. Maggie gave her another shot, and bathed her again with alcohol.

When Sina was once again quiet, Ward left the room, eased out the back door and went down to the barn. He had never before got down on his knees to pray, but he did this time—on the hardest place he could find!

"Lord," he said, simply and directly as if he was looking Him straight in the eye, "please don't let her die. She is doing too much good work down here for you to forsake her and let her precious life be cut short. If you should have it in mind to punish me, Lord please don't do it this way…

"Anyway, Lord, I haven't been all that bad…I have taken lives only when I've had to save those I love or myself. As for those I have killed in battle, surely, Lord, you wouldn't hold it against me or Sina for taking part in a just war to end the evils of slavery.

"So please, Lord, spare her life. Not just for me, but for the good she can do and inspire in others during the rest of a normal life span. And, Lord, I promise to do all I can, too. Amen."

He got up, rubbed his knees and went back to the house that he and Sina had so lovingly planned and helped put together. As he was quietly tiptoeing back into the room where his "treasure" was lying, he shouted for joy when she looked up at him with instant recognition!

He took Sina's hand in his and kissed her cool cheek. Her fever was back to normal. The crisis was passed. His beloved Sina was going to live!

"Hey, Girl," Maggie said as she came running, "you even had me worried there for awhile. But if you'll now stay in bed until I say you can get up, you'll soon be as good as new. Ward," she went on, "I want you to see to it that she follows my instructions to the letter."

"Don't worry about it, Doctor," Ward assured her with a stern look at Sina…he well knew how headstrong she could be.

They all laughed when Sina said in a wee small voice, "Please, may I now have a little sip of water?"

"Yes, of course," Maggie agreed, "but just a sip, and not anymore for an hour.…But if you are still feeling this chipper at sunup, you can have some chicken soup.

"Now," Maggie added with a smile, "if I can borrow a night gown— one that's kinda big 'round th' middle—and one of your bedrooms, I'll go take a nap."

Everybody laughed as Laura fetched a gown from the closet, and then showed the exhausted doctor and expectant mother to a bedroom.

*   *   *

A week later, as Juan was driving Maggie back to town after she'd been down to remove Sina's stitches, she got to thinking about the life-altering decision she had made...

Actually it had been a decision she had been forced to make by the scurrilous stories Evan, Jr. had kept on spreading around...stories that went way beyond the truth, and were certainly unworthy of a man who wanted to be thought of as being a "Lord-of-the-Manor" gentleman.

She had at first not even thought about "exiling herself" to Brushy Creek. But one day when she was thinking about Ward, as she often did, the idea had popped into her head. She knew in her heart there was little chance of winning Ward away from Sina, but she could find out if their marriage was as solid as everyone thought it would be. If she found out that it was, she'd back off and no real harm would be done.

Since she had arrived in Brushy Creek, she had come to realize that—aside from the slim chance she had of winning Ward away from Sina—there had been another reason in the back of her mind for choosing a "nowhere" town way out on the wild frontier. It was because the more she had thought about Ward and Sina, the more she had realized that they were genuine people of character, and the best folks she had come to know—especially when compared to the poor specimens of mankind she had known around Marlin....If she found them to be truly devoted, she'd gladly settle for the chance of making them her good friends...

She felt some strong kicks in her tummy, and shifted her position to ease the pressure she'd been putting on little Johnny.

Chapter 24

Sina was sitting out on the veranda in an easy chair, convalescing and taking in the grand view she had come to appreciate even more since her recent brush with death. Ward was puttering around the barn waiting for Juan to get back from town with the supplies he'd gone for. When his loyal hired hand finally returned, Ward could tell from his solemn manner that he was worried about something.

"Meester Ward," he said, as he stepped down from the buckboard, "I see my cousin in town, and he tell me Boss Clark has hired a very bad man to keel you! He is Charlo the Breed, and he send word you must meet him tomorrow mornin' in town for a showdown, or he will keel the first Garrison he see!"

Ward felt the hackles start rising on the back of his neck...to be told that Charlo was calling you out, was like hearing the tolling of one's own death knell!

"One other thing," Juan went on, "my cousin say he hear Charlo has a new trick he might use...somethin' about a peestol that can keel a long way off...."

Ward nodded his thanks as Juan turned to unharness the horses.

He had heard about the gun slinging 'breed before he'd gone off to war. He had even seen him a couple of times around Brushy Creek...probably at times when he was laying low between "jobs". He'd heard several grisly stories about the half-breed who had set out to "out-Indian" the fiercest warriors on the plains in violence and blood-shed. From what he'd heard, Charlo had more than succeeded.

It was said that at fourteen he had killed his own father, a white trader who had failed to keep a promise he had made to an Indian girl. Charlo had buried his tomahawk up to its haft in his father's back!

Sam Packer, the white trader who had long since forgotten the Indian girl with whom he had dallied, had slumped to the ground and died with no chance to plead for his life or to promise amends.

A year later, Charlo left the tribe and began passing himself off as a Mexican. After two years of free lance robbing and stealing, he had learned that killing white men for other white men, and sleeping in a white man's bed every night, was a lot more profitable and comfortable than stealing from dirt-poor settlers and sleeping on the hard ground.

He had moved from town to town, and in each town he had let it be known that his deadly gun was for hire. And in nearly every town he would soon be hired by somebody bearing a grudge, someone who wanted what someone else had, or someone who wanted somebody put out of the way.

And now, in the hire of Bascom Clark, Charlo the Breed had issued his deadly challenge to him…a challenge Ward had to meet or see some member of his family shot down.

But a thought came to mind…the new U.S. Marshal, maybe he'd do something. But when Ward rode into town to talk to Marshal Gilchrist, the circumspect political appointee said, "Sorry, Ward, I can't do a thing until I have reason to think that a law has been broken."

So much for Ward's well-intentioned effort to prevent more bloodshed…

The next morning, after having thought about it most of the night and not being able to figure any way out, Ward told Sina he had to go to town for something he'd forgotten to tell Juan to get the day before.

It was hard for him to do, but he gave her the same warm parting kiss he always gave her when she knew he'd be back in a few hours. When his kiss proved to be routine enough not arouse suspicion, he went riding off without Sina suspecting that she might never again see him alive.

Rob joined Ward at their parents' place…not for any treacherous scheming on their part, but to review their plan to forestall treachery from the hired killer's side…like being on guard against a second gunman backing Charlo's play.…

On their way into town, Ward, for the second time, reminded Rob to make sure nobody shot him from th' top of Bob Garner's saloon.

"With you shootin' from a rest with that old Henry rifle," he went on to say, "you ought t' be able to pick a backup killer off at a hundred yards, even if he's showin' no more than his head."

Rob nodded, and said, "Don't worry, Ward.…Nobody is going get a clean shot at you from any rooftop, or from a corner of any building.…I'll make sure it is a one-on-one fair fight."

From the edge of town they rode behind stores and other places of business until they came to the back of Tom Logan's store. They stopped their horses there, and Ward made preparations to defend himself against some special "peestol" the treacherous Charlo might use against him.

First he put on a longer than usual coat, and then pulled the short-barreled Winchester from its saddle boot. He tied a leather thong to the stock of the rifle, and then put a loop in the thong big enough to go over his head.

With the loop around his neck, he positioned the rifle so that it hung muzzle-down behind his back where it couldn't be seen from the front. With his bandanna hiding the thong, he was ready…as ready as he reckoned he could be.…

He couldn't help smiling at the irony of it all.…He remembered how he had dreamed during the war of coming home to good ol' peaceful Brushy Creek, far from war and killing. But now, after four years of bloody war—and being lucky enough to get back to his beloved hometown alive and well—he was still having to kill or be killed!

They heard a stir up the street, and when they moved up to the front of Tom's store they saw a crowd gathering around the front of the saloon, which was across and up the street a ways.

"Damn!" Ward said, "I was hopin' this could be done without drawin' a crowd…I don't like bein' made part of a big spectacle."

There was another stir in the crowd and they knew that Charlo was about to make his "entrance". After pausing in the saloon doors to build suspense, he finally stepped out on the sidewalk to greet his "audience" with a wave and a big smile.

They watched as the 'breed, with cocksure bravado, sauntered on out into the street as if he was aiming to do nothing more that demonstrate his prowess by quick drawing his gun and shooting any luckless bird that might come flying by.…

Thinking that he might put a little kink in his tail, Ward stepped out in the street and called out, "Hey, Charlo, do you want to be buried in a silk-lined coffin like a white man? Or had you rather be laid out Indian-style on top of some ridge for th' buzzards to eat?"

"Ah," the 'breed said as he squared around to face Ward, "I'm glad you come out of hiding…I hate havin' t' run a man down to keel him. I like keelin' brave men…I don't feel so—how you say—geelty for doin' eet."

So much for his attempt to get Charlo's goat.…The 'breed might be crazy, but he had the confidence of a man who knew he was the best at what he did.

Ward wiggled his shoulders to make sure his rifle was still in the right position, and started moving up the street toward the cocksure 'breed.…

He saw that Charlo was wearing one of his fancy, eye-catching out-fits: Black hat with a mottled snake-skin band, an Indian-made vest with beaded designs, and fancy, hand-stitched boots. All to show every-body that Charlo the half-breed may have been born in a teepee on some barren, windswept plain, but he had come up in the world! He could now wear fancy hand stitched clothes just like a white man!

Ward scanned his fancy garb for suspicious bulges, but he saw no sign of any weapon other than the .45 he was carrying in a holster tied low on his right thigh....But of course he couldn't see what the canny 'breed might have stuck in his belt behind his back.

With slow, deliberate steps, Ward moved steadily toward the 'breed, while the 'breed moved just as slow and steady toward him.

When Ward had counted ten steps, he knew he was still fifteen yards beyond the accuracy range of a standard .45. If Charlo had a special gun, he knew the next few yards were critical....He knew he could easily kill the 'breed with a rifle shot from where he stood, but if the 'breed had no long range pistol, that would be turning a fair fight into murder....All he could do was watch Charlo's every move and be ready to instantly respond.

With the secret edge that Charlo knew he had, and thinking that he'd catch his quarry off stride, in the middle of Ward's next step he went for his gun.

Ward saw his move, reached back for his rifle and dived to the ground. As he was going down he got a glimpse of the long-barreled pistol the treacherous Charlo had drawn from his holster. The extra six inches of the double-length barrel had been stuck through the open end of the 'breed's holster and on down through a slit in his pants leg. The longer barrel made it accurate up to twenty yards farther than a regular .45.

He felt a tug on his left sleeve as he was going down. But before the 'breed could get off another shot, he fired his rifle from where he was hugging the ground...when the slug from his rifle tore into the 'breed's right side, Charlo's knees sagged and the long barrel started drooping.

Ward levered in another shell, but he saw there might not be any need for it. As long as that barrel didn't start coming up, he'd save his lead. Anyway, the vicious little killer deserved to die slow and in much pain. Charlo finally slumped to the ground and started inching himself along toward a nearby wagon.

Ward stayed low and worked his way over to a horse trough by the sidewalk. From the horse trough, he crept along the creaky walkway toward the wagon with his finger on the trigger every step of the way....There might still be enough life in the little half-breed for him to get off another shot.

He finally worked his way up to where he could get a good look under the wagon....Charlo was lying in a spreading pool of blood with his long-barreled gun lying beside him. Ward knew that he could very well owe his life to the vital information Juan had brought him.

Still on guard with his gun cocked and ready, he eased around to where he could see both of the 'breed's hands. When he saw that neither of them was holding some other secret weapon, he relaxed and moved in closer. He was about to prod the little killer with the barrel of his gun, when Dr. Maggie Carson came rushing up with her little pill bag.

With no thought for her swollen pregnancy, she immediately crawled under the wagon and opened the little killer's fancy vest. She was hard-put to maintain her professional composure when she saw the blood that was gushing from the hole in the side of his chest.

"That bullet must have splintered a rib and the pieces ripped up his liver," she grimly diagnosed. "There is no chance of saving him," she gravely concluded, as she pulled his vest back over the gaping wound.

"Good," Ward snorted, "if you had said there was, I'd have put another bullet in him!"

"Oh, Ward," Maggie chided, "don't talk like that."

"Hell, Maggie!" the keyed-up ex-captain of cavalry lashed out at her, "there's no tellin' how many good men that crazy 'breed has killed!...If I hadn't been lucky enough to put an end to him here today, who knows how many more men he would've killed, includin' me!"

At the sound of Ward's loud words, the dying 'breed moved his head and his eyes fluttered opened. His wavering gaze finally settled on Maggie's face, and he put his hand up to touch her raven tresses.

"Make fine scalp," he murmured as his eyes closed in the death he deserved twenty times over!

"Did I forget to mention?" Ward smiled sarcastically as he eased the hammer down on his rifle, "that he never hesitated to scalp a woman."

"Touche," Maggie grunted, as she scrambled out from under the wagon. "Come on," she urged, "you need a drink and so do I...never have I seen so much blood come out of one body!"

Rob joined them for a quick bracer, served up by Bob Garner who was making no attempt to hide his disappointment that Ward had been the victor in the shootout with Charlo.

They all noted Bob's insulting show of partisanship, but they didn't let it stop them from lifting their glasses in solemn gratefulness that Charlo had been unsuccessful in his attempt to add Ward's scalp to his growing collection. When they had drained their glasses, they smashed them on the floor in an up-your-nose gesture to the insolent barkeep, and swaggered out through the swinging doors.

After pushing through the crowd that had gathered around the wagon to stare at the dead 'breed, the Garrison brothers walked Maggie back to her office, and then went on to where they had left their horses.

No word was spoken between them, but they both knew that their lives, as well as every other Garrison's, was still hanging in the balance...and would be until Bascom Clark was brought to heel.

Chapter 25

Sina was furious!…at first, anyway. But she finally had to admit that Ward had simply done what had to be done. Had their roles been reversed, she knew that she would not have told him that her chance of ever coming back would be no better than 50-50.

With every breath she took for the rest of the day, she gave thanks to the Lord.

To get away from Indians, half-breed killers, power-crazed range lords and deranged killers of all stripes the thought of them all moving back to Illinois came to mind. She immediately chided herself for thinking such a thought. She knew that she could never leave Brushy Creek, and she knew that wild horses couldn't drag Ward out of his beloved hometown!

Jo and Laura had been taking turns staying with Sina and doing her heavier household chores during her recovery period. When she had finally been allowed to get out of bed, Dr. Maggie had given strict orders not to let her do anything strenuous. A week after Ward's shootout with Charlo, she let her start riding a few minutes each day, with her solemn promise that she would mount her horse from the side porch, a stump, or some other place that would "give her an easy leg up".

After another week of obediently following instructions, she was allowed to ride as much as two hours every other day. She continued to do as Maggie said, but she was itching to get back into some real action…roping yearlings, dragging them up to the branding fire, and hanging on to the saddle horn when her horse had to dodge the horns of a hostile bull.

One day after they had had their lunch, Jo helped Sina saddle up for another one of her doctor-allowed rides. Jo watched her out of sight and then went back in the house to take up where she'd left off in the book she was reading…

An hour or so later, in the warmest part of the afternoon, Jo laid her book aside and strolled down to the creek. She loved to go there to gaze at the big pool of cool, clear water. It brought back memories of her childhood days on the plantation when she and two friends would slip down to the bayou and go skinny-dipping. She smiled at the happy memory and decided to take a quick dip in the secluded pool.

She slipped out of her dress and waded out into the cool water of the spring-fed creek. When she had become used to the cool water on her legs, she waded out into a deeper part of the pool and started swimming and splashing around like she and her friends had done during those stolen moments at Hampton Wood.

She was finally getting used to the feeling of being free and secure…she was so pleased to be in Brushy Creek with Josh and her good friends, away from the sting of the lash and belittling abuse at the hands of cruel, uncaring people…

Her lithe brown body glistened in the sun as she turned gracefully in the water like a playful mermaid. She was a sight to turn any man's head, be he white or black. But Jo was innocently unaware of her head-turning allure, and continued to playfully cavort in the cool, remote pool, never dreaming that she was stirring the passions of a vile wretch that was ogling her from hiding.

She swam to shallow water, stood up to brush her hair back and glory in the pure pleasure of being young, free, and alive. The areolas around the nipples on her breasts showed through her wet chemise, and droplets of crystal clear water sparkled on her bronze thighs.

The sight of her standing in the sun like that, stirred the ignoble cad's passions even more. And with no effort to control them, Wesley Clark slithered out of hiding with a leer on his face, and said, "Well, if you ain't the prettiest little chocolate drop I ever did see. In fact, I ain't never seen one of your kind with her clothes off…no wonder them clodhoppin' farmers fought so hard to hold on to their slaves…come here and let me see if you feel as good as you look!"

Jo was paralyzed with fear, but she came alive to the danger she was facing when the leering, sex-crazed brute dropped his pants and came wading toward her! Knowing that the leering brute had rape on his mind, she ran through the water and on up the bank to where she had left her dress.

With trembling hands she groped for the little derringer that Josh had given her. She managed to get it out of the pocket of her tangled up dress just as Wes was lunging up the bank only a few feet away. She cocked the little gun and pointed it straight at him, but with groans of primal passion and his eyes fixed on her golden breasts, he kept coming at her.…

She first aimed the little gun at his chest, but it not being in her gentle nature to kill, she lowered her aim before she squeezed the trigger. Her bullet struck him in his right thigh and put a halt to his brutish attack.

Wes grabbed his thigh and started yelling obscene curses with no thought for how glad he should be that she hadn't shot him in his heart..

With his passion giving way to more profane curses, he half swam and half waded back across the creek. He struggled up the bank, grabbed up his pants, and limped back to where he had tethered his horse.

When he had slipped his pants back on, and had pulled himself up in his saddle, he shouted back at Jo, "You'll be sorry for this, you black bitch!…You'll pay dear for shootin' a white man!"

With her hands still trembling, Jo put her dress and shoes back on as quick as she could and ran back to the house. Twenty minutes later, Ward and Sina found her lying on a bed, still in near panic, sobbing and trembling.

Sina gathered her in her arms, and said, "Jo! What's happened?"

She was finally able to stop sobbing long enough to tell them.

"Oh, how I wish I had killed that little bastard back on the trail!" Ward groaned in regret. "But," he went on, "better late than never.... If I hurry, maybe I can catch him in town."

"No!" both women cried out at the same time. But Ward knew the little weasel deserved no mercy...he needed to be shot!

"Come on," Sina said to Jo when she saw that Ward wouldn't heed their pleas, "we'll go along with him...we want to get the true story of this outrageous assault on the record as soon as we can, anyway."

The women were relieved but Ward was disappointed when Justice of the Peace, Ollie Norton, told them that Wes had already sworn out a warrant for Jo's arrest, and had then "lit out" for to the Circle C.

"He probably knew," Ollie gave Ward a sidewise glance, "that you'd be comin' after him."

"Yeah," Ward growled, "the little weasel was right about that....Now," he went on, "who are you goin' t' believe?...Jo or that peepin'-tom, woman-assualtin', sorry excuse for a man?"

"Well," Ollie dodged Ward's question, "you know I ain't one to take sides. 'Specially not in this fight that's goin' on between you Garrisons and th' Clarks. So I'll just let the circuit judge handle th' matter when he comes t' town next week. Meanwhile, I'll release this woman in your recognizance, if you'll promise to be responsible for her appearin' in court."

"That won't be any problem," Ward promised.

Chapter 26

The certainty of a sensational, lid-blowing trial had stirred so much interest and strong—even hostile—feelings that it was moved from the small J.P. Court to the much bigger saloon so a larger crowd could be accommodated.

The J.P.'s bench and high-backed chair had been brought in from the J.P. court, and more chairs had been brought in from homes and businesses. The earliest comers got the chairs, the late comers had to stand up. But chairs were reserved up front on each side of the aisle for the Clarks and Garrisons, just like the front pews at church.

The regular judge had died a few months before, and that set Ward to wondering if Bascom already had the new judge in his pocket like he'd had Judge Simpson. For Jo's sake, and for the sake of justice in general, Ward hoped the old tyrant had been too busy hassling the Garrisons to find time to "work out an agreement" with the new judge.

To Ward's dismay, it was plain to see from the start, that hardly anybody was sympathetic to Jo—who was generally referred to as "that nigger wench". He knew that many folks were believing that Wes may have been "getting his jollies" by ogling her, but she had been deliberately teasing him. But whether or not she really was, according to their reasoning, the comely wench had no business being in the creek cavorting around with no clothes on.

Wes limped up to the witness stand, grimacing with every "painful" step, and perjured himself a dozen times with his blatant lies. Ward watched in disgust as the all-male jury swallowed every one of the little weasel's bald-faced lies and then glared at Jo!

The San Antonio lawyer that Josh had hired, put Jo on the stand to tell the truth of the whole matter. But even though her friends were all there supporting her, the glowering Clarks kept staring her down. And her testimony, given in her naturally soft voice, was not forceful enough to displace any of the wrong notions the jurors already had locked in their minds. And of course the toady prosecutor Bascom had put in office, got her all mixed up in his cross examination and made her story of the humiliating event sound even weaker.

In an effort to help Jo all they possibly could, Ward and Sina asked to be allowed to take the stand as character witnesses. They told of Jo's gentle nature, her flawless character, and how it would be impossible for anyone who knew her, to believe she would shoot Wesley Clark simply because he had stopped to water his horse—as he had so falsely testified.

Their testimony on Jo's behalf may have helped a little, but when the jurors came filing back in after "deliberating" less than ten minutes, they could see on their faces what the verdict was going to be. They knew, of course, that they could appeal, and they grimly intended to do so. If need be, they'd spend every penny they had to get her a fair trial.

"Has the jury reached a verdict?" Judge Larkin asked. —Judge Larkin was the judge that had taken Judge Simpson's place.

The foreman of the jury quickly rose to say, "Yes, Your Honor, we have."

But before he could say what everybody knew he was going to say, Diann Clark suddenly stood up, and said, "Your Honor, I have to say something…I can't sit still any longer."

Judge Larkin rapped his gavel to restore order and said, "Why, of course, young lady, if you think you have something that is material to this case, come forward and be sworn."

Ward, like everyone else in the room, was wondering what the hell was happening....He looked across the aisle and saw that Bascom and Ursula seemed to be just as shocked as anybody. But then he saw her daddy relax and he figured that Bascom was taking it for granted that Diann was going to add some testimony that would absolutely seal the case for the Clarks, and add more years to Jo's sentence.

When Diann had been sworn in and had seated herself in the witness chair, Judge Larkin took over the questioning.

"Now, young lady," he spoke kindly, "what is it you want to tell us?"

"Well," Diann said, without looking at her parents, "what my brother Wesley said was all lies! I saw the whole thing, and it wasn't like he said at all!"

The courtroom exploded!

Judge Larkin had to pound his gavel for more than a minute before he could restore any semblance of order. Finally he said, when everybody had quieted down, "Go ahead, young lady. Tell us what you saw."

As her stunned parents stared in mounting disbelief and growing anger, Diann said, "Jo—Mrs. Anderson—was in the creek swimming, all right, but she did not have all of her clothes off, and she did nothing to entice Wes. He was riding by and happened to hear her splashing around. When he did, he got off his horse and slipped down to the creek to see who it was. When he saw it was Jo, he hid behind some bushes and started ogling her.

"But he soon came out of hiding," the courageous girl went on, "said some insulting things to Jo, and told her to come to him. When she didn't respond to his insulting request, he started wading out toward her with an awful look on his face.

"Mrs. Anderson ran to the bank where she had left her dress, took out a small gun and pointed it at Wesley. But even with her pointing the gun at him and telling him to stop, Wesley wouldn't stop...not until she shot him in the leg.

"Your Honor," Diann looked earnestly at the old judge, "Mrs. Anderson actually spared his life, because she had first pointed the gun at his heart, but she aimed it at his leg before she pulled the trigger. And now she is facing prison for attempted murder...Your Honor, that's not right!"

"That is quite a different story," the old arbiter said. "Tell us," he went on, "exactly where you were when you saw all of this?"

"Up the creek behind a tree, only a few yards away," she candidly replied.

"And could you tell us how you came to be at that particular place so far from home?" the Judge questioned.

"Yes, Sir," Diann lifted her chin, "since we knew my father would never approve, Robert and I have been forced to meet secretly in out-of-the-way places. This was one place where we sometimes met. But let me add, Your Honor, for those who might want to brand me as being a loose woman, I was always properly chaperoned."

"This Robert you mention, did he see all of this, too," the judge asked.

"No, Your Honor, he had not arrived at that time," Diann replied.

"Would you please tell us this young man's last name"? the judge kindly requested.

With her love shining bright in her eyes, Diann looked straight at Rob and said, "Yes, Your Honor, his last name is Garrison."

The courtroom exploded again, but most folks kept their eyes on the front row where Bascom was sitting.

"You disgraceful little slut!" he bellowed as he leaped to his feet, livid with rage. "How could you dishonor your family like you've done, and then so blatantly flout your disloyalty before the whole town? You are no longer a daughter of mine...I disown you! You've made your bed with Yankee trash, so go lie with them and **die with them!**"

Ursula had glared at her daughter throughout Bascom's angry tirade, and had nodded her head in agreement with everything he said. With one last angry glare at her disloyal daughter, she grabbed up her crutch and went crutching along behind Bascom as he stormed toward the door, glaring angrily at anyone who dared to meet his eye.

"Hold Wesley Clark," the judge ordered the bailiff, "I'm sentencing him to a year in jail for perjury."

Upon hearing the judge's order, Bascom turned to shout, "Don't worry, Wesley....We'll have you out of there in no time, and there won't be enough of this town left for th' buzzards to say grace over—especially th' nigger-lovin' Garrisons!"

With that grim promise, Bascom led his clan through the swinging doors and on out to their fancy rigs.

When the last member of the infuriated Clark Clan had stormed from the courtroom, Judge Larkin banged his gavel until order was again restored.

"I hereby dismiss the charges against Mrs. Anderson," he proclaimed, "and I remand Wesley Clark to the city jail where he will start serving his sentence. Meanwhile, we'll see what other charges ought to be lodged against him. —I think we can start with attempted rape...

"I am also appointing Ward Garrison an officer of this court to see that my orders are carried out, and to see that order is kept in this town." With a nod to Ward he went on to say, "Take charge of the prisoner."

And with a bang of his gavel he brought to a close the most memorable session of court ever held in Wollock County!

Chapter 27

Ward put a vise-like grip on Wes' arm and steered him to the door. Meanwhile, all of Jo's other friends were rushing to hug and congratulate her. With that done everybody then turned to Diann.

Rob and Laura put their loving arms around her as Mary Wilson came rushing over to say, "Diann, Honey, until preparations for a wedding can be made and properly solemnized, you can stay at my house."

With tears on her cheeks, Diann smiled and thanked her.

"And don't worry about clothes," Mary told her, "as you know, you and my Amy have worn each other's clothes ever since your early school days. I'm sure she'll be glad to share them with you until we can make you some more."

Amy caught Diann's eye and smiled a friendly affirmative.

Sina and John had given Jo a quick hug and had then hurried out to guard Ward's back as he escorted the detestable Wesley to jail. When they arrived at the jail, Ward asked Abel for the jail keys and he handed them over without any protest. Ward then told him that he was relieved of duty, and had to stay away from the jail until further notice.

Abel had heard the judge's order, and he didn't offer any objection to that either, but he left with a smug look on his face....He had heard Bascom's angry threat at the saloon door just as everyone else had, and he fully expected to be back in charge of the jail very soon...where he'd very likely be the turning the key on Ward—if there was enough of him left to lock up!

After giving Wes a careful search, Ward locked his still-cocky prisoner in the one-cell jail. As he was turning the key in the lock Wes warned, with an insolent sneer, "In th' end, Big Boy, it'll go a lot easier for you if you turn me loose right now."

Ward stared at the little scourge of the county with his hunched-up shoulders and weasel eyes, and said, "You better not let your mouth run on too much, Wes. 'Cause if you start me to thinking you might get out of this without going to Huntsville for fifteen or twenty years, I might do to you what you'd do to me if our roles were reversed."

Wes' sneer turned into a puzzled look that faded altogether when he finally understood what Ward had said.

The town's new peacekeeper dropped the keys in his pocket and went back to the jailer's office to make sure there wasn't some duplicate keys lying around. But before he left, he sat himself down to do some hard thinking....

The trial had indeed ended in a totally unexpected way. But as pleased as he was that justice had been rightly served, he knew that the trial's tumultuous end was only a prologue to what could be happening in a few hours. He had seen the rage on the old range lord's face, and he knew that his threat should not be taken lightly.

Some preparations should be made, even though the best defense he and the townsfolk could put together would have little chance against the gang of gunmen Bascom could marshal against them....He wished for a seasoned troop of cavalry he could lead in a quick swoop on that nest of scofflaws. He'd wipe them out before they could even get their boots on!

He thought about Marshal Gilchrist and the help he could provide. But the marshal had left town the day before to attend some government function in San Antonio. Nobody knew when he was supposed to be back. Ward couldn't help wondering if he had deliberately left town when he saw trouble brewing....Maybe he should give the new marshal some credit for having sense enough to make himself scarce when he saw that the whole town could explode in his face at any minute!

He went outside to talk the matter over with John and Sina. They agreed that Bascom and his lawless gang would sooner or later be coming back, bent on storming the town, and ready to blast anyone who tried to stop them from breaking Wes out of jail.

John had just got through saying that he doubted if Bascom could get his troops together for an assault that night, when Juan Vasquez came riding up at a gallop and slid from the saddle before his horse had skidded to a full stop....

"Meester Ward," he said, with his face all pinched up in a worried expression, "I just got word from my cousin, Tomas, that Meester Clark ees comin' tonight, and he say he ees goin' t' burn thees town and hang ever' Garrison he can catch!"

"Oh, Hell," Ward groaned, "that doesn't give us much time to make plans and get ready...so I guess we'll just have t' do th' best we can...

"The first thing we have t' do is to keep Bascom from knowin' that we know he's comin', and th' plans we'll be makin'. . . which means we'll have to roundup his spies and lock 'em up. Come on, we can start at the saloon."

Thanks to Juan's warning, he'd have a little time to organize some semblance of defense that would give everybody a chance to fight off the vicious attack rather than being massacred in their beds.

With John and Sina standing by, Ward paused to look over the swinging doors to see who might be in the saloon. He saw no Clark henchmen other than Bob Garner who was busily pouring drinks for a line of townsmen standing shoulder-to-shoulder at the bar. It was an easy guess: To drum up support for Bascom, Bob was pouring free drinks for any man that bellied up to the old whiskey-soaked slab.

He guessed that the bootlicking barkeep was looking past the minor battle Bascom had just lost, and was cherishing the thought of how his old boss would, within days, win the war and dominate Brushy Creek more than ever. He knew that Bob Garner would do any underhanded thing he could to help Bascom get rid of the "meddlesome, Yankee-loving" Garrisons.

He shoved the doors back, walked over to where the Clark toady was pouring free drinks, and said "Bob, put that bottle down, keep your hands where I can see them, and come out from behind that rat nest you call a bar…you are comin' with me."

"Can't you see I'm busy?" Bob protested, "I have a room full of patrons with big thirsts for good whiskey."

"Don't worry about your thirsty patrons," Ward told him, "just come along with me and don't start any trouble…"

Bob glanced at his shotgun as he reluctantly came out from behind the bar, but he wisely thought better about making any move. Ward made him hand over his keys and then patted him down for a gun he might have hidden somewhere in a secret pocket.

When the last grumbling freeloader had more or less voluntarily left the premises, John closed the shutters, and Ward locked the main doors.

He was agreeably surprised when he stepped out on the sidewalk and saw Abel Gunderson and Billy Hatcher standing on the far side of the street. (Billy was out on bail pending trial for framing Josh.)

"Well," Ward called out to them, "I was just wondering where I might find you two…you've saved me th' trouble of runnin' you down. Drop your gun belts and come along with me."

Knowing that Ward was now an officer of the law—temporarily, at least— they shucked their guns and joined the collection of Clark spies that Ward would be putting out of action for the night.

The three of them protested every step of the way and kept telling Ward how sorry he was going to be when they told Bascom about the highhanded way they'd been treated.

Ward prodded them back to the jail cell, unlocked the door, shoved them in and relocked the door. Wes, acting as if he had just been retained as their hotshot defense attorney, got up on his hind legs and "hurrumphed" to know why "these good citizens" were being locked up.

Ward stared at Wes and the other three for a long moment and then said, "Just do some thinkin' on it and it might finally come to you."

"Now," Ward said to Sina and John when they were back outside, "with one more boot-licking spy behind bars, we'll have a chance to make some preparations without Bascom getting word of our every move."

"Yeah," John nodded his head, "and I bet that one more you are thinkin' about, is the preacher, Homer Bisbee."

"He's th' one," Ward said, "so why don't you take th' buckboard out to his house and bring him in?…Hold up your right hand and I'll deputize you."

"Hey," John laughed, "I'll bet you are the first son who ever made his daddy an officer of the law.

Chapter 28

Thirty minutes later, with twenty of the town's leading citizens sitting around tables in the saloon, Ward was telling them about the assault that Bascom Clark was aiming to launch against them and their town in just a few short hours...

"But," he said, "if everybody pitches in to help, we can set up a defense that will give us a good chance to save our businesses and our town."

"I don't know about that," one man spoke up, "as I see it, this is a fight between you Garrisons and the Clarks...why should th' rest of us be drug into it?"

"It's true," Ward said, "that we Garrisons are at odds with th' Clarks. It's true, because we Garrisons had rather fight Bascom Clark than let him rule our lives. But if any of you had rather go on lettin' him bully you around, and don't want to help defend your town, you can get up and leave....But I warn you, if you are caught tryin' to help th' Clarks in th' comin' fight, you'll be treated as one of them."

Five of the twenty got up and walked out. Ward hadn't expected so many to tuck their tails and run. (He made a mental note to post a guard on the road to stop one of them if he tried to run and tell Bascom about the defenses they'd be setting up.) With him, John and Rob, plus Josh and Juan added to the remaining fifteen, there'd still be twenty defenders and they might not be outnumbered by more than two to one…he'd do his best with what he had.

He reminded the fifteen who'd stayed to fight to wear dark clothes, make sure they had plenty of ammunition, and to clean and oil their guns.

"About your ammunition," he told them, "if what you have is not fresh, Tom Logan says he'll let you have some at his cost—on credit. He also said he'd lend a gun from his store to any of you who don't have one that's dependable." He didn't tell them that he'd had to promise Tom that he, or his estate, would pay for any gun that was damaged, or for one that wasn't returned.

He went on to tell them that he had a surprise in mind for Bascom and his cutthroat crew. A surprise that he was sure would go a long way toward evening the odds in their effort to save their homes and loved ones from a rapacious mob.

"Now," he continued, "after we have done some things around here, all of you go home and fill all of your barrels and other big vessels with water, and then get out your ladders and some extra buckets so they can be put to quick use. And don't forget to tell your wives and kids to stay home, and keep out of sight.…Be back here before dark so we can all take up our positions and be ready."

As Ward was leaving the saloon he was met by a group of citizens that had gathered out front. From the look on their faces he knew he was being confronted by more townsfolk who were afraid of taking a stand against Bascom.

"Why don't you end this threat to our town by turnin' Wes loose? He ain't really done nothin' to be locked up for," a worried bigot suggested.

"Of course he ain't" said another one, "nobody believes what that nigger wench says. And since that girl of Bascom's had already turned against her family, why should anybody believe her?"

"How can any of you," Ward spoke calmly, "be sure that Bascom in his towering rage will spare your house, or even your life?"

"Oh, he knows who his friends are," an ex-saloon girl said.

"Yeah," a third man spoke up, "and like Jesse and Benny said, I'm not ready to help a Yankee family and their friends save their property, just because some nigger wench bared her butt to Wes!"

"All right," Ward said, "then stand on th' sidelines and do nothin' for your town if you are so inclined. But don't get in our way unless you are ready to be treated as an out-and-out ally of the Clarks."

With glares and grumbles and warnings as to what was going to happen to those who turned on Mr. Clark, the sullen group broke up, and went clomping off to homes that might be nothing but heaps of charred rubble when the sun next rose.

To Ward's dismay, he had seen three women in the group who were wives of three men who had stuck with him in the saloon. If the husbands of those women deserted him, only seventeen men would be left to defend the town against thirty or maybe even forty of Bascom's freebooting scofflaws.

But they had to make a stand. A line had to be drawn. If they could hold out long enough, maybe news of their resolute stand would reach San Antonio, and bring troops to their rescue.

The seventeen loyal defenders first carried all of the tables and chairs out of the saloon and piled them in the street to start a barricade. Then, while the others went about town picking up anything that could be used to build the barricade higher and wider, four men joined Ward in setting up his surprise. He desperately hoped it would work. He expected his defenders to be outnumbered by more than two to one, but the surprise, if it worked, should narrow the odds.

Two men went to the livery stable and soon returned with a load of hay. The other two went to get coal oil from the store, rip some pickets off fences, and gather up some feed sacks to make torches. With that done, they joined the group that was still gathering junk and scrap for the barricade.

Tom Logan wouldn't give Ward the key to the cellar where he stored his blasting powder, but he loaned him a wrecking bar he could use to break the lock. Ward helped himself to a keg of powder, and with Josh holding each bag, he poured a big pound of it in each of the fifty paper bags he had "borrowed" from Tom's store.

Fence-straddling Tom hadn't volunteered to give the defenders anything, or to do any fighting. But knowing that Ward would take what he needed at the point of his gun, he had agreed to sell supplies to the "foolhardy" defenders at his cost. He was hoping Bascom would spare his store…he was banking on him remembering that he got a big reduction on everything he bought there.

When the street was covered with hay all the way from the west end of Main Street up to the barricade in front of the hotel, Ward had the men pour coal oil on it so it would ignite instantly and burn fast. By the time that was all done, the sun had gone down and night was coming on.

Ward thought about the guns in the office at the jail, and hurried there to get them. As he was re-locking the office door he heard a rider coming fast from the east end of the street. He turned to look and saw that it was Marshal Gilchrist returning from San Antonio. Good, he thought, with the Marshal now present, and with Bascom knowing that a U.S. Marshal could call in troops from the Army, he might pull in his horns and no house would be burned and nobody would be hurt.…

When the marshal saw Ward he reined his horse in, quickly dismounted, and said, "I've heard what you are doing.…Have you gone out of your mind? Do you want to start another war and get a lot of folks killed?"

Before Ward could give him an answer to either question, the fuming marshal went on to say, "I've been told what happened, and I can't believe you are endangering this town by holding Wesley Clark on such a minor charge? Give me the key so I can release him, and then ride out to the Circle C…maybe I can get Bascom to forgive what you have done to him and his family."

Ward said, "Marshal Gilchrist, Judge Larkin made me an officer of the court and told me to jail Wesley for contempt. He also told me to keep order in Brushy Creek, and protect it the best I can. So I am just doing my duty as the judge ordered."

"You were ordered, you say. Well, where is that order? Let me have a look at it," the marshal demanded, his broad face still flushed, and the ends of his moustache still twitching.

"It was a verbal order," Ward told him.

"A verbal order?" the marshal scoffed, "that's no good. —I'll have to see it in writing."

But before Ward could reply, the marshal looked at the darkening sky, and said, "…But if Bascom should already be on his way, I'm afraid there won't be time enough for you to find the judge and get one.…So hand over that key, so I can let Wesley out in time for us to intercept Bascom before he gets here, and see if he'll settle for an apology."

Ward reached under his coat but it wasn't a key he pulled out. It was his gun. He leveled it at the Marshal's belt buckle, lifted his gun from its holster, and said, "No, Marshal, I'm goin' to do my duty as ordered. Anyway, as riled up as Bascom is, I'm sure he'd come on and wreck our town even if you met him on th' road with a boot-licking apology.…We have a good defense organized, and we are goin' t' do th' best we can to stop him…to keep you from interferrin', I'm lockin' you in your office until this thing is all over."

He turned the Marshal around, prodded him in the back and said, "Move."

Over his shoulder the red-faced marshal said, "Don't you know what this could mean?…Keeping a U.S. Marshal from doing his duty at the point of a gun in an occupied zone?…it could mean life in a federal prison."

"Yeah," Ward grunted, "if it does, then I say better there than spendin' the rest of my life in a town under Bascom Clark's heel."

He marched the checkmated marshal to his office and made him open the door. He then tied and gagged him and left him lying on the floor.

"If I come through this alive," Ward promised the trussed-up marshal, "I'll get Judge Larkin to write out an order and I'll bring it you."

At the end of another half-hour, Ward had his loyal but sure to be out-numbered defenders in position. He reckoned they were as ready as anyone could expect shopkeepers, corn grinders, barbers and boot menders to be, and would put up a good fight.

But he was hit by another stinging disappointment. Three of the fifteen men besides "his family" were no where to be seen. Their desertion would probably increase the odds against them to about three to one.

The missing three were the husbands of the three women he'd seen in the protest group in front of the saloon....Ah well, he shrugged his shoulders, maybe some men just hadn't been born with enough fortitude to stand up against a man who would destroy everything they owned—even their manhood and self-respect.

But their loss wouldn't make all that much difference. Two-to-one odds were already pretty overwhelming. But what the heck, he had risked his life dozens of times fighting for a cause that wasn't half as close to his heart as this one. He squared his shoulders, offered up a silent prayer, and vowed to make Bascom pay, and pay dearly.

He smiled with mixed feelings of pride and dismay, when he remembered telling the men to instruct their wives to stay home. He and John had tried to be "gallant" husbands and fathers, too. But they could have saved their breath for all the good it did. Neither had it worked on a spunky girl who had given up everything for her man.

Diann had stubbornly insisted on standing by her man instead of riding off to San Antonio as Ward had suggested. The women of the twelve men who had staunchly stayed to defend their town stood by their men, too.

After warning everybody to stay away from the section of street that was covered with the oil-soaked hay, Ward and Josh brought out the fifty bags of blasting powder. They carefully placed one under each of the fifty mounds of oil-soaked hay that had been randomly spaced on the hundred yards of street that led up to the barricade.

With that all done and everyone else in position, he and Sina picked up their unlit torches, climbed to the top of the saloon, and took up their position behind its false front.

When they were settled in place close beside each other, Ward looked at Sina with her black 'boggin cap pulled over her glorious blond hair. He could barely make out her lovely face under the black soot, but he could tell that she was looking at him, too. He took her in his arms, held her close, and kissed her.

When he finally pulled back from his loving kiss, he said, "You've done a good job of blackin' your face, but if I see you exposing yourself too much, I'm gonna slap you down and put my foot on you!"

Sina smiled up at him, and said, "It's nice to be loved so much."

She pulled his head back down and kissed him with all the love of all the devoted women who had stood by their men from the time-blurred past right down to the perilous present. If this day was to be their last on earth, then so be it…it would just be the end of their first eight and a half months of eternity together.

Ward responded with all the love of all the good men who had loved their loyal women down through the ages….Could any man ever be a complete man without the love of a good woman?

They held hands as they waited in the dark, remembering their long ride down the trail to Brushy Creek…holding hands from saddle to saddle with stars in their eyes, never dreaming that their future was loaded with so many perils. Ah, but they had faced them all together and, up 'til then, had overcome every one.

Sina prayed for help in overcoming this one, too, and for it to be the last deadly peril they'd ever have to face. There was a lot of life to be lived, and worthwhile things to be done—like raising a family. She was still hoping to become pregnant, but the only father she would ever want for her babies was Ward.

Ward was sure that Bascom was hoping to catch everybody asleep, and had ordered his horde of cutthroats to keep quiet so they could pounce without warning. But he hadn't thought they would actually be so quiet, and would get so close before he heard them. They were already at the end of Main Street when he heard a horse snort....Bascom and his hired guns were only moments away!

Ward got set to strike a match and light the first torch.

With the silence broken by a fretful horse, Bascom immediately signaled the charge. Horses were spurred into gallops, guns were drawn, and the horde of nightriders began pouring bullets into every house they galloped by.

"War Lord" Bascom had arrived, and he wanted every Brushy Creeker to wake up and suffer his wrath! He wanted them to never again forget that he was Lord and Master of Wollock County!

Ward waited until the first riders were well into the hay-covered section of the street before he threw his first torch. Sina's threw hers a second later. And a second after hers, more torches came arcing out from the roofs of other buildings, to ignite more of the oil-soaked straw and set off the bags of blasting powder. In less than five seconds the would-be surprisers had themselves become victims of surprise.

Only moments before, men who knew no pity and were hell-bent on spreading panic and destruction, were now being blasted from their saddles. The street had become a wild scene of struggling men and frantically surging horses, all eerily illuminated by the burning straw.

Bascom tried desperately to rally his men, but with more bags of blasting powder exploding around them, they ignored his profane orders. They had been told that they were going to "tree" a sleeping town, break Wes out of jail and quietly hang a couple of Garrisons in a dark alley. They had also been told that they could have "their way" with a few women, but nothing had been said about them having to ride through an exploding hell of blasting powder!

Every man who was still on a horse, or could grab a stirrup and haul himself back into a saddle, ran out on the old range boss. He was left sitting on his horse in the middle of the street surrounded by flames and explosions!

Any man in control of his senses would have spurred his horse into a desperate dash for the end of the street. But showing his backside in fainthearted retreat didn't fit the image the haughty old range baron had of himself.

Instead of him tucking his tail and running, he pulled a second gun from his cummerbund and defiantly brandished it over his head. And then, with a gun in each hand, he rode up and down the street firing into the windows that were now reflecting the flames of the fires…the dry goods store, the shoe shop, the hotel, the general store. But he seemed to get the most satisfaction out of firing shot after shot through the windows in John Garrison's office.

As he'd been riding back and forth, defiantly firing his pistols, five more bags of powder had exploded in the street around him. But as if some invisible shield sent from Hell was protecting him, he had not been blown from his saddle.

When the lordly old baron had emptied his guns, he halted his horse at "center stage" and started reloading them with a big show of arrogant bravado. While he was so theatrically engaged like some haughty old actor playing to a lowbrow audience that was incapable of appreciating his performance, he was blasted from his saddle by a load of buckshot!

His arms flew up and he toppled from his saddle into a patch of burning straw. And while everybody was still looking at the self-centered old tyrant with varying degrees of concern, his tunic started smoldering, and a few moments later his beard caught fire!

John and Josh couldn't be sure the last bag of powder had exploded, but without hesitation they ran out to drag his body away from the flames....Even though his soul had long since departed, the body in which it had once resided deserved some respect.

As they were approaching the old range lord's body, they caught sight of a body lying close to it. It was the remains of Bascom's oldest son, Tom. He had been one of the first to be blasted from his saddle, but he had landed in a spot blown clear of burning straw.

Nobody would ever know, of course, whether or not Bascom knew that Tom had fallen. Some folks thought he had, and the sight of his son lying in the flames, had triggered a wave of regret for the harsh, loveless way he had raised his sons. They believed that the wave of regret had brought on a disgusting feeling of remorse, and that had triggered his determination to put an end to it all in the time honored way of all betrayed monarchs...death in his saddle with hostile foes, fell by his own hand, lying all around.

Bascom's end hadn't been exactly like that, but in his last "royal" moment, he was probably content with the thought that he had dispatched a few of the "baseborn simpletons" that had tried to dethrone him.

To his way of thinking, feeling remorse meant that he was getting old and weak....Which, in turn, meant that he might as well be dead. So he had made use of the stage that had been so conveniently set up for him, and had made an exit worthy of the grand monarch that he had seen himself as being.

John and Josh barely had time to pull his smoldering body from the path of a buckboard that suddenly burst out of the darkness at the end of the street. Everyone gasped when they saw that it was Ursula who was driving the wild-eyed horses into the blinding flames...

As she kept on lashing the terrified horses through the fires and explosions, while she stood on her one leg with the mummified remains of her other leg hanging from a rope around her neck, her intentions became all too clear to those who were watching in helpless dismay....Ursula aimed to end a miserable, unrewarding life with a grand exit of her own!

John and Josh tried to stop the wild-eyed horses, but with their bits in their teeth and their nostrils flaring, they charged right past them. Unfortunately, because of the fires in the street, the terrified horses couldn't see the barricade.

Ursula came down in the midst of the tangled wreckage and the pitifully mutilated horses. Cries of horror went up from those who had just witnessed a woman that had become embittered with the life she'd been dealt, and was hurling it back in the face of a heartless, uncaring world!

*   *   *

When Bascom first appeared "on stage" with his "noble-monarch" act, Rob and Diann had been watching from the front of the general store. But when Rob foresaw the inevitable end to her father's theatrics, he immediately led Diann to Tom's office in the back of the store.

When they heard the doomsday blast of a shotgun, Rob felt Diann go tense in his arms.

"Somebody just shot him, didn't they?" Diann's words sounded more like a statement than a question.

"Yes, I'm afraid so," Rob whispered as he held her close.

He was still holding Diann in his arms when they heard the crash of the buckboard and the ensuing gasps. With feelings of dread they rushed to the front of the store.

By the time they reached the horrible scene, Ursula had already been lifted from the wreckage and carried to the sidewalk. Diann cried out in anguish when she saw her poor mother's broken body. She rushed to her side, sat down beside her poor, abused mother and took her in her arms.

Ursula's wandering gaze finally came to rest on Diann's face, and through bruised and bleeding lips, she whispered, "My darling little girl. How I wish I could have been a proper mother to you."

Her eyes then closed for a long moment, as she seemed to be gathering strength to say more. With a painful effort, she finally opened them again, and said, "Please, Diann, find my leg and bury it with me, so I can once again be a whole woman."

Diann whispered softly in her ear, "Yes, Mother, I will."

Ursula smiled and closed her eyes in peace.

Chapter 29

Ward stood up and surveyed the aftermath of the battle from the saloon roof. As captain of the town's defenders, he was pleased that his plan of defense had worked so well. Especially so, since, from his vantage point, he could see that every member of his beloved family had survived Bascom's onslaught. And as far as he could tell, much to his amazement, so had all of the other town defenders.

He was not proud of the casualties that had been inflicted on the other side. But when an implacable enemy declares war on you, you have to fight back. And since one of the best ways to win a war is to destroy the enemy's will to fight, he felt justified in having used in an innovative way the destructive means that happened to be at hand.

He went on to reason, with some justification, that far fewer casualties had resulted in the brief though violent battle, than in a nightlong battle with guns. Anyway, he was not about to start feeling guilty over the fact that all of the casualties appeared to be on the other side.

"Come on," he said to Sina, "let's go join the others, and make sure they are all right."

They were approaching the hotel, and were only a few steps from the awful scene where Ursula had ended her unrewarding life, when Jo came running out of the hotel with an anxious look on her face.

"I was just goin' out to look for you," she said, "come quick, Judge Larkin has been hurt!"

Ward's heart sank. He should have known that no battle could be fought with casualties on only one side, no matter how innovative the victorious commander might've been.

He kept hoping for the best as he followed Sina and Jo into the hotel and on up to the judge's room. They found the old judge lying on the bed with Dr. Maggie holding a bloody towel to his side.

"What happened? How bad is he hurt?" Ward asked.

"He was up there in the lobby when that awful man was ridin' back and forth, shootin'," Jo told him. "One of his bullets hit him!"

"Damn!" Ward pounded his fist in his palm, "why have I always been so hesitant about blasting a Clark?"

"Because you always try to avoid killing anyone," Sina was quick to console him.

Maggie looked up and said, "He's losing blood fast...the bullet ruptured a vein....I'll have to make an incision so I can get in there and clamp it off."

As she was opening her bag to select a scalpel, she looked at Jo, and said, "Go get Maria Sanchez...I have started having birth pains. I think little Johnny is coming a bit early...I hope I can stop the judge's bleeding before the little early bird demands my full attention."

Ward suddenly remembered that he needed an order signed by the judge, and that meant that where he spent the rest of his life depended on the old judge's survival!

"How can we help?" he asked Maggie.

"Take this gauze," she said, "dampen it with chloroform and if he shows signs of becoming conscious, hold it over his mouth and nose for a few seconds just like you did with Sina."

To Sina, she said, "Take these retractors, and when I make the incision you hold the sides of it back."

She made an incision with one smooth stroke and while Sina retracted the sides, she found the vein that was gushing blood. She quickly clamped it off and started closing the ugly tear with some deftly inserted stitches.

She tried to hold it back, but she couldn't completely muffle her moan of pain. She asked Ward to hand her a towel, and she quickly put it between her legs to catch the water that could break at any moment!

Ward knew that his future was hanging in the balance....If Maggie should pass out before she had the vein fully stitched, he would not have a chance to get the order he needed to satisfy Marshal Gilchrist. No chloroform had been necessary to keep the judge unconscious, and that was a bad sign...the old jurist was well up in years.

Maggie grabbed her stomach again and groaned with pain.

Ward wondered if he should tell her of the situation he was in? He could have kicked himself for even thinking about it. —Putting more pressure on Maggie at a time like that would be an unworthy thing for him to do.

Maggie's water broke, but after a short pause she took a deep breath and went on with her stitching.

Jo returned with Maria just as Maggie was tying a knot in the last suture that was needed to seal the vein. She sponged the blood out of the incision, told Sina to take away the retractor, and started stitching the incision. After one stitch she looked at Sina and said, "You saw how I did that...you put the rest of them in, about a half-inch apart."

Jo helped Maggie to a daybed over in a corner, and while Maria tended to her, Sina put six more stitches in Judge Larkin's side. While she was bandaging his wound the old arbiter opened his eyes and they could see that he was conscious—for the moment at least.

Ward leaned over the old judge and told him that Dr. Maggie had stopped the bleeding, and that he was going to be all right. He then told him about the written order that Marshal Gilchrist was demanding.

He could have shouted for joy when the old judge spoke in a much firmer voice than he had expected.

"You write it out," he said, "and I'll sign it."

Ward wrote out two of them and the judge signed them both. It was an effort for the old judge, but Ward saw that his signature was perfectly legible on both copies.

As he was putting them in his pocket, Sina gave him a reproachful look and said, "You didn't tell me about Marshal Gilchrist."

"No, Darlin'," Ward said as he took her hand, "I figured you already had enough to worry about....You stay here while I go show this to th' Marshall and cut him loose...this is no place for a man at a time like this, nohow."

Except for him being angrier than a maverick bull that had just been castrated, Ward found the marshal right where he had left him. He lit a lamp and while he was removing the gag he had crammed in his mouth, he held a copy of the judge's order before his eyes.

"Yes, but is there any of this town left?" the angry marshal asked. He was of course referring to the loud blasts he'd heard.

"Every bit of it," Ward assured him as he cut his hands loose, "all of th' little explosions you heard were just small bags of blasting powder to slow Bascom's charge. Our town has survived his onslaught. He is dead, his wife is dead, his oldest son is dead and Wes is in jail. The mighty Circle C has been dehorned and deballed!

"By th' way," he went on, "when you write out your report, I think you should include **all** of the facts and tell th' whole extenuatin' truth about this matter, because a lot of this town's goodwill depends on how you put things.

"It's too bad you missed your chance to make yourself look good to your bosses....Instead of runnin' off to San Antone when you saw trouble brewin', you could've stayed around to keep th' lid on things, and make a name for yourself all th' way up to Washington...

"But if you word your report just right, you can still come out of this without lookin' too bad....If you'll forget about me havin' to tie you up at a critical time, I won't say anything about you runnin' out on your job when you saw trouble brewin'."

At the door Ward turned back to say, "For your information, I have another signed copy of the judge's order in my pocket, and it reads exactly like yours."

*   *   *

From the marshal's office Ward went on down to the jail. As he stepped up to the office door he reached for the ring of keys on his belt, but the door was already open…

"There are three guns pointed at your back, Big Boy…as quick as you are, one of us will get you for sure if you go for your gun."

He turned around slow and saw in the dim light that it was Wes Clark, Bob Garner, and Abel Gunderson. It was Wes who'd done the talking.…He should've known Bascom would bring along a handyman who could pick a lock and smuggle Wes a gun. The little weasel was right. With their guns already cocked and leveled, he wouldn't have a chance.

What a sad turn of events.…When was that fickle genie gonna get off his back? For the last thirty minutes he had been feeling like a hero and was looking forward to a long, happy life, but now he was going to lose everything to a scabrous, unworthy little villain.

He knew that he was very close to death.…He could get one of them, but one of the other two would surely get him. Waiting for a better chance sure couldn't make things any worse, and with the little villain savoring his opportunity to lord it over him, he didn't seem to be in any big hurry to finish him off.

"So," the scabrous little villain went on, enjoying every moment of his new-found "sovereignty", "just drop your gun belt and step over here."

When Ward had done as he was told—as slowly as he dared—Wes went on with his order-giving, "Abel and Bob, you go find some horses.…Just three," he added with a smirk, "Ward won't be needin' one 'cause he is gonna be sproutin' wings…but until then I might have some use for him."

When the two toadies had gone to find three horses as Wes had ordered, he said to Ward, "You thought you had whipped the Clarks and was rid of them, didn't you? Well, as you can see you didn't whip 'em all, and you sure ain't rid of me…

"In a month's time, everybody in this county will be sayin' Sir to me and tippin' their hats when I ride by. It's too bad you won't be around to see it. But your family will—especially that cute little wife of yours—'cause she'll be ridin' high in th' saddle with me.

"And," he went on gloating, "just to add a dash of color and variety, I may add that little chocolate-drop friend of yours to my list of good-time girls."

Ward clinched his jaw and fought hard to control himself. He wanted to charge the little viper and grind his face in the dirt. But he held himself in check and waited for a better chance…

That better chance came when Homer Bisbee—who'd been on his knees in the cell giving thanks for his deliverance—said from the door behind him, "Bless you, Wes, for…"

Ward instantly slashed Wes' hand with the keys….the bullet that was meant for him tore through Homer Bisbee's throat!

Before Wes could cock and fire again Ward wrenched the gun from his hand. Then, with the little villain cringing before him, Ward said, "I'm goin' t' strap my gun back on and give your gun back so you'll have a fightin' chance…"

But Wes had another gun, and he started easing it out of his pocket. Ward almost didn't see it in time.…

As Wes was reeling back with a .45 slug in his gut, Ward said, "That was for the thoughts you were having in your dirty little mind about Sina and Jo!"

There'd be no "Sirs" or tipped hats for Wesley Clark! The best he'd be getting was an otherwise useless little rock to mark his grave.

Ward was stooping to see about Homer when he heard horses coming fast down the street. When their riders were close enough for him to be sure who they were, Bob Garner was already putting his shotgun to his shoulder. Ward shot him out of his saddle before he could pull the trigger.

He would have done the same to Abel Gunderson had his horse not reared and dumped him on the ground. Lucky for Abel, by the time he'd got up and started running, Ward had changed his mind. As much as Abel deserved to be shot, Ward couldn't pull the trigger on him.

With a weary sigh he dropped his gun back in its holster. He was sick and tired of killing, and hoped he would never have to kill again.

Everyone at the hotel heard the shooting at the jail, and they all came running with terrible feelings of dread. But when they saw Ward still standing tall, everybody smiled and breathed prayers of thanks.

As he was holding Sina close, he said, "Someone see about Homer....He wasn't aimin' to, but he saved my life when he said something from the door that distracted Wes...he caught th' slug that Wes was aimin' t' put in me."

Homer Bisbee was dead. He had sold his soul to Bascom Clark, and had reaped his reward.

"Come back to the hotel," Sina said, as she tugged at Ward's sleeve, "I want you to see something."

When they were back in the old shot-up hostelry, Sina led him back to Maggie's room. She was lying on her bed with a big smile on her face and a red-faced baby in her arms.

Ward smiled and said, "Is he all right?"

Maggie and Sina laughed, and then Maggie said, "She's not a 'he', Ward. But we can still call her Johnnie...we'll just have to change the 'y' to 'ie.'"

Ward laughed along with everyone else, as he looked down at his little daughter...

"That's all right," he said, "even if we do have to spell her name with 'ie' instead of a 'y', we'll love her just th' same."

With a sober look on his face, he asked, "How's th' judge?"

"He is going to be all right," Maggie smiled, "when they were carrying me out I had them wait while I felt his pulse…it was beating strong and regular."

"That's fine," Ward said, as he looked at Sina. They both knew that Maggie had not only saved Judge Larkin's life, she had also saved Ward's.

What a friend the Good Lord had sent them! How could they ever repay her?

As Ward was taking one of Maggie's hands in his, Sina was taking the other one in hers. And while Sina was smiling with tears her eyes, Ward told Maggie how glad they were that she had come to Brushy Creek. He then told her how she had saved him from life in prison by saving the judge.

With her eyes full of tears, Maggie looked up at them, and said, "I'm glad I was here to do it…both of you just keep on being my good friends."

Chapter 30

With Rob at her side, Diann made all of the arrangements for getting her family's mortal remains back to the Circle C for burial. In any normal family a daughter who had just lost her whole family in one evening, would have been totally devastated and unable to handle the arrangements.

But of course Diann's family had not been a normal family. She had literally been forced **not** to be a real part of it. She'd been taken from her mother the day she was born and, for the most part, had been ignored by her parents and brothers all of her life. But a wise surrogate mother had loved and nurtured her, and she had made the most of her chance to get a good education—and learn from a schoolteacher a set of good values to live by…that teacher, of course, had been Laura Garrison.

Rob and Diann were married two weeks later in the Brushy Creek church. And since Homer Bisbee's misplaced "fealty" had brought him to an untimely end, Ollie Norton, the town J.P., had tied the nuptial knot.

Amy Wilson had of course caught Diann's bridal bouquet.…Had she been blindfolded and whirled around three times she couldn't have missed it because Diann threw it straight into her arms. After a big reception at the hotel, the just-marrieds rode off to San Antonio to celebrate their honeymoon.

They were back a week sooner than they had planned, telling everybody that they had started proceedings to sell the Circle C to three wealthy Englishmen. With the proceeds from the sale they said they aimed to build a house in town, and buy Tom Logan's store.

Ward strongly opposed their plan to sell. He told Rob he should advise Diann to hold on to the ranch. As the main ramrod, he could become a mighty big man and make her even richer…

Running a big ranch, he told Rob, was the manliest business a man could get into…owning and controlling all of the land you could see in any direction, grazing thousands of cattle, building a ramuda of blooded horses that would be second to none, organizing and directing the efforts of a hundred men. —To say nothing of being recognized by other men of standing anywhere he went in the whole state.

But Rob knew that Diann had too many bad memories, so he just grinned his easy-going grin, and said, "Ward, I agree with Diann that selling out is the right thing to do. We have thought long and hard about it, and I don't think we can be persuaded to change our minds."

Ward threw up his hands, and said, "All right, it's your life." And with that he stomped out of the room.

Of course Sina had been hearing Ward's strong sentiments on the subject every day since Rob and Diann had come back with the news that they intended to sell. But every time he got started, she just smiled her little Quaker smile and kept her peace.

In the meantime, as little Johnnie's proud godparents, they had been visiting her nearly every day. And of course Laura and Jo were at Maggie's room in the hotel nearly every day, too, cuddling and holding her.…Ward was all the time grumbling that the women were spoilin' her rotten, but once he got her in his arms, it was all but impossible to pull her away from him.

A month after Rob and Diann had decided to sell, the papers were all signed and sealed and the deal for the Circle C was closed. They broke ground for their new house the next day, and began working on the deal for Tom Logan's store.

One bright sunny morning a week or so later, Ward and Sina saddled up for a ride into town to visit the newly weds, and to see how their fine new house was coming along.

Ward was not yet fully reconciled to Rob giving up his opportunity to become a big rancher. But he had consoled himself by stoutly declaring that since Rob wouldn't do it, he would take it on himself to make the Garrison name paramount in the ranching business.

He had talked every day for two weeks about how he aimed to hire more hands to put the Bar G brand every longhorn they could flush out of every mesquite thicket for ten miles around. When they had rounded up two, maybe three thousand head, he'd drive them up Kansas way to some railhead.

With the money he made, he'd buy more breeding stock, put them in fenced pastures, and start developing a beefier, more profitable herd…high-grade stock that could soon be driven to a railhead in San Antonio, just twenty miles away. In just a few years he'd be just as big if not bigger than Bascom Clark had been!

Once again Sina sat patiently through it all as they rode the first mile up the road toward town. When Ward stopped Buck to gaze out over his favorite vista, and picture in his mind the empire he was going to build, Sina stopped her horse beside his, and said, "Ward, you know I love you, and want you to be happy more than anything in the world.…That is why I must say some things that I feel in my heart.

"I don't doubt," she went on as he turned to face her, "that you can do all of the things you've been talking about because you are intelligent, a natural leader, a hard worker, and a good manager. And you certainly have all the drive you'd need to reach any goal you set for yourself.

"But to become the big man you're talking about, you'd have to ride roughshod over a lot of good folks, and make enemies out of other men who'd be just as determined and relentless as you in battling their way to the top.

"You will always be trying to cook up another big deal, and you'll finally have so many irons in the fire you won't have any time for your family. But you will never be satisfied no matter how many gambles pay off, or how big you get. You'll always be setting new goals, looking for bigger deals to cut, and gauging your success—even your happiness—by the bottom line on your balance sheet.

"Finally, with all of the pressure you'll be putting on yourself to stay on top, you'll become another Bascom Clark!...Feeling as if you have to control everything around you, eliminate every little threat, compromise on nothing, and bully everybody into abject submission....And just as Bascom did, you might even fly into a rage and vent your wrath on a whole town just because something didn't come out exactly like you wanted it to.

"Would that be somebody you'd want our little Johnny to grow up to be like?...I'm sure you don't want that. So will you please promise not to set your mind too hard on building the state's biggest cattle empire, and not leave yourself time to enjoy the dearest possession you'll ever have?"

After thinking for a moment that he might have dozed off, he suddenly sat up in his saddle, and said, "Did you say **our** little Johnny?"

When Sina smiled her little Quaker smile he whooped with delight and sailed his old Stetson clear over the moon!

He swung down from his saddle, took Sina down from hers, and held her in his arms for a long, long time.

Finally he said, "Sina, Honey, I regret all of the big talk you've had to put up with, and I'm glad you've made me see what it could lead to. I promise you won't be hearin' any more of it....You are giving me what I really want, and I sure don't want our little Johnny growing up to be like Bascom Clark, or anybody like him."

He sat her back in her saddle and after he'd retrieved his hat he swung back aboard Buck. When he was settled in his saddle, he looked over at his little treasure, and said, with a teasing smile, "OK, you little

man-manipulatin' genie. If I know you, you already have another plan
for our future all mapped out....One in which we won't be workin' our
tails off ropin' and brandin' longhorn mavericks....So out with it...let
me hear it."

"Well," she said, as she flashed another one of her little smiles, "I
don't want to give up the Bar G and the home we both love....And I
want little Johnny to grow up here just as I know you do. But I believe
my plan will help us develop our full potential, and put us on the road
to fuller, even more satisfying lives...

"I read in the paper awhile back that they now have a law school in
San Antonio....That started me to thinking that a good knowledge of
the law would help us develop our potentials, and do more for our
country....I'm sure your daddy would let us live in one of those nice
houses he inherited from his uncle, and we could hire a reliable maid to
mind Johnny while we attend classes.

"Juan, with your other two hands, could handle all of the normal
chores at the Bar G, and we can come back every two or three weeks to
check on things, rest from our studies, and renew our spirits. Little
Johnny would soon learn to love it just as we do, and would start putting down some "tap roots" of his own."

Ward didn't respond to the notion of his wife going to a higher
school of learning in the way most men would have responded. He was
too broadminded, and Sina had many times demonstrated her quick
wit and natural intelligence. He knew that her intelligence far exceeded
most men's, maybe even his. She deserved more education, and the
chance to be all that she could be. Besides, with all of the new towns
springing up on the frontier, Texas would be needing a lot more
lawyers...

The longhorns they didn't want to keep, they'd sell to the new owners
of the Circle C....Juan and his two helpers could very well run a scaled
down Bar G just as Sina had suggested...raising cattle and turning out a

modest number of high quality breeding stock that more and more ranchers would soon be clamoring for....

And come to think about it, it would be a lot of fun watching Sina argue a case in a courtroom...especially against some range baron like Bascom Clark who was forcing some poor nester off land that he had homesteaded, cleared and nurtured....Or against some railroad company that was cheating homesteaders out of their proved-up quarter sections...or some heartless slave owner who had not really freed his naive chattels. Lord help any poor devil that found himself in a situation like that...Ward smiled as he remembered poor Mr. Babson up in Arkansas.

He looked at Sina, grinned and said, "Well, I know who, in no time at all, will be the junior partner and who'll be the main ramrod with her name on top of our letterheads...but it's a deal. Ten years from now we'll be headin' up the most famous law firm in th' state!"

"There you go again," Sina laughed, "setting big goals and wanting to be King of the Hill...let's just settle for getting you elected to the state legislature, and then maybe to Congress."

"All right, I'll settle for that," Ward said as he leaned over from his saddle and kissed the best woman that had ever stood by her man through hell and high water. Before settling back in his saddle he looked into Sina's eyes, and said once again, "What a treasure thou art!"

They held hands and rode on up the road, side by side, stirrup to stirrup, looking to a future free of war, violence, and bloodshed.

As they neared a bend in the road where it came close to a willow thicket that grew along the creek, they heard riders approaching from around the bend....It was probably John and Laura coming for a visit....But no, there were more than two horses. There were four, maybe five. They exchanged glances and stopped their horses to wait....

They were a little puzzled when they saw five soldiers in Yankee blue come riding around the bend...an officer, a sergeant, and three privates.

They had been hoping that a U.S. Marshal would be the only "occupation force" they'd ever see in Brushy Creek…

Ward's heart froze in his chest when he saw that the officer was Major Dundren—the highhanded Commander of Occupation Forces they had left all trussed up in a horse stall in Benton, Arkansas!

Ever since he and Sina had ridden out of Benton, anxiously looking over their shoulders, he'd had a nagging dread of the day when someone would come along putting up wanted posters for he and Sina.…Was that what Major Dundren and his troops were doing after all this time?…putting up wanted posters all the way down to San Antonio and beyond?

He doubted if it was. It would be much easier to send them out from San Antonio on the new stagecoach.…Maybe the Major had been reassigned, and was in the area for some other reason. Maybe to survey the Brushy Creek area for a good place to set up an Army outpost to keep Indians at bay?…Could it be possible that he had forced himself to forget the embarrassing incident in Benton, and wouldn't even recognize him and Sina?

That forlorn hope immediately vanished, when a change in the Major's bearing clearly indicated that he had recognized the "pair of hooligans" that had violated his person and had left him all trussed-up in a stinking horse stall!

Ward was sure the Major's reaction meant that he had indeed come looking for them, and his sole purpose for riding down a road that led only to the Bar G was to put them under military arrest! Ward glanced at Sina and saw that she had also recognized the arrogant Major.

"He has come to arrest us," he whispered to the love of his life, "but if we let him do it, we'll be murdered long before we ever see a courtroom in Benton. He knows he'd be laughed at in court, and he couldn't stand that.…He aims to have his revenge by putting bullets in our backs somewhere along th' trail on th' way back.

"So we can't let him take us.…But let's wait and see what he has to say. If he says anything about arresting us, we'll take as many of them with us as we can…but I'm claimin' the Major for myself."

Sina nodded, and said, "I'll get as many of the others as I can…"

"So we finally meet again," Major Dundren greeted them with a mocking, thin-lipped smile, as he stopped his troops two horse-lengths away, "I see you are still riding a horse that belongs to the U.S. Government." He wasted no time in indicting Ward.

"Well, Major," Ward drawled, "I figured I needed him more than you did. I would've been left on the trail without one, while there were plenty other horses in the corral for you."

He'd keep the egomaniac talking as long as he could to give he and Sina a few more precious moments…

"Yes," the Major smiled his thin-lipped smile again, "but none of them had the qualities of the horse you were riding. A Commander of Occupation Forces has the right to claim the best available, you know."

He was about to raise his hand and give the command, "Arrest them!", when eight renegade Indians came whooping out of the willows to rudely interrupt the Major's vindictive command.

Ward knew the Indians were after horses, his and Sina's as well the Major's and his troopers', and that made the Indians a mutual enemy.…To have any chance of surviving the sudden attack, he and Sina would have to join forces with the Major and his troops.

When he saw the panic on Major Dundren's face, his instinct for command took over and he shouted, "Take cover in the draw!"

But only he, Sina, and Major Dundren made it to the draw beside the road.…They made it because he and Sina had dropped the three savages that were leading the charge, while Major Dundren had been clinging to his saddle on the offside of his horse to shield his precious person from the Indians' arrows.

Four of the remaining Indians immediately grabbed the reins of the four rider-less army mounts, and went racing back to the willows, hazing ahead of them the three horses their dead cohorts had been riding.

Ward was lining up another shot when Sina, just in time, saw Major Dundren leveling his gun at Ward's back. She shot the major in his left side, exactly in line with his black heart!

Ward winged one of the fleeing Indians and then turned to say, "I think four horses will satisfy them…I don't think they'll be comin' back."

When he saw Sina staring over the barrel of her still smoking gun, he looked to where it was pointing. He then saw the Major's pistol and the direction in which it was still pointing.

"You mean," he said, "that low-down ungrateful bastard was about to shoot me in th' back!"

Sina nodded her head as she lowered her gun…she was glad she had kept her eye on the treacherous wretch!

"Thank you, my love," Ward said, "for once again savin' my hide."

He then turned his attention back to the willow thicket, looking for signs of another arrow-launching charge. But instead of any sign that the marauding savages were getting ready for an another attack, he heard them crossing the creek and heading west. One casualty per horse was not a good deal, even an Indian could figure that.

So the fight was over! They had miraculously dodged death from two quarters! —the Indians and Major Dundren! They had once again eluded death against big odds.

"Please God," Sina prayed, as she put her gun away, "let this be the last time."

Ward went to check on the four downed troopers. They were all dead with arrows sunk deep in their chests. When he got back to the draw where he, Sina, and the Major had found cover, his eyes suddenly became fixed on the bullet hole in Major Dundren's jacket.

"Oh, Hell," he moaned, "I'm sorry to have to tell you, my love, but we'll have to give up the great plans we just made! When Marshal Gilchrist sees the bullet hole in the Major's side, he'll know an Indian didn't kill him. And from th' mere fact that we'll be th' ones who report the Indian attack, he'll guess that we were here when it all happened, and that'll make us his prime suspects! With th' hard feelin's he's harborin' against me, he won't listen to th' truth, and will lock us up for th' murder of a U.S. army officer!

"By doing a little checking, he'll soon find out about the trouble we had with the Major back in Benton, and that'll make his case even stronger. So we have to head for the border right now!

"We can pick up some things we'll need at the ranch and then ride south as fast as we can. We have to put all the distance we can between us and the posse that'll be comin' after us."

"Oh, Ward, I'm sorry. But there was no other way..." Sina sadly lamented.

"Of course there wasn't," Ward consoled her, "and I'm not forgettin' that I owe you my life," he went on to say as he took her in his arms for a quick embrace.

After a quick kiss on her cheek he said, "Come on, we have to get movin'. Every minute counts...somebody is sure to have heard our shots.

"Our shots!" he groaned bitterly, "isn't it all crazy? We save th' bastard's life without him firin' a shot! Then when he is about t' shoot me in th' back, you have to shoot him to save me. And now we have to run to Mexico to save our necks!...how could things get so mixed up?"

The bright future they had so joyfully planned had suddenly turned into a crazy nightmare!...A hellish dream in which they were being forced to ride off into a strange land to eke out a bare existence among barely civilized people who had little love for Texans!...What was even worse, little Johnny would have to grow up there in some squalid little town with no school, no doctor, and no hope for his future.

Sina was desperately trying to think of the things they needed to pick up at the ranch when Ward suddenly halted Buck in his tracks, and said, "Wait a minute… maybe we don't have to run to Mexico and leave all of our dreams behind…come on, lets get back to that draw."

When they were back at the shallow draw beside the road, Ward quickly dismounted and started looking around. He soon found what he was looking for…an arrow that had missed its mark and ended up in a soft bank. He pulled it out, cleaned it off, and brought it back to where Major Dundren had died in a dishonorable effort to soothe his bruised ego.

He located the hole Sina's slug had left in the vainglorious Major's side, pushed the arrow point through the hole in his jacket, and then shoved it all the way down into his rotten heart!

"Now," he said, as he looked at Sina and saw the promise of a great future lighting up her precious face again, "who will ever know that the 'gallant' Major didn't go down with his troops when they were viciously attacked by a band of renegade Indians? Who won't believe that we came riding to their aid as fast as we could, but, regrettably, we didn't arrive in time to be of any help to the 'brave' Major and his men?"

The lovers for all time fell into each other's arms and held each other very close for a long, long time.

The full, happy life they had envisioned only minutes before, had suddenly gone black and left them facing desolate lives as fugitives in a foreign land. But now, thanks to Sina's watchful eye, and Ward's bold, resourceful thinking, their future was once again bright.

Finally, they relaxed their embrace and leaned back to look deep into each other's eyes. With love that was eternal, both of them said at the same time, "What a treasure thou art!"